The Kingdom of Munndora

KIM ROGERS

AUTHOR AND ILLUSTRATOR

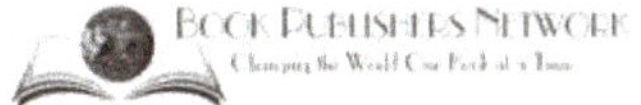

BOOK PUBLISHERS NETWORK
Changing the World One Book at a Time

Book Publishers Network
P.O. Box 2256
Bothell • WA • 98041
Ph • 425-483-3040
www.bookpublishersnetwork.com

10 9 8 7 6 5 4 3 2 1

Printed in the United States of America

LCCN   2019914977
ISBN   978-1-948963-38-1

Editor: Julie Scandora
Cover design: Laura Zugzda
Interior design: Melissa Vail Coffman

To the many people who inspire the lives of others. To my loving parents, Roy and Lucille, my brothers, Brant and Gary, my loving nieces Marieka and Larissa, and their families.

MANY YEARS AGO, there was an exotic kingdom south of Scotland called Munndora. It was west of Calve Island on the northeastern coast of the Isle of Mull. This kingdom was famous for its export of nutritious, premium produce and other plants grown there. Other crops harvested there helped strengthen livestock. Munndora grew strong in that part of the world because of its shipping business, including importing products such as the newly discovered cocoa and coffee. It was said the crops grown in Munndora were so rich in nutrition that they had magical powers to create romance and mend broken hearts. The mysterious ways of Munndora gave wonder and curiosity. Some have said the people of that kingdom had superior strength and intelligence. Unfortunately, what was once a beautiful kingdom is now deserted and barren. Little is known what happened to Munndora. Some valuable log documents were lost during the last years of the sixteenth century, but this we do know. The kingdom of Munndora was known as the land of truth.

* * *

THE MIGHTY KING BREVE ruled over this land. His son, Mochaba, was raised learning the skills of leadership. He loved riding horses and especially thrilled in a fast run on horseback.

On the morning of Mochaba's fifth birthday, the king said to him while sipping the last of his cup of coffee, "Son, your mother and I have a gift for you. Walk with me to the stables."

Anything having to do with horses really excited Mochaba, and he happily accompanied his father. The king talked with Mochaba as they walked. When they reached the corral, Mochaba saw a young colt happily playing and jumping around his mother, the king's mare. Showing the love of being alive, the colt ran with enjoyment and excitement with his long and lanky stride. When he saw the king and Mochaba walking up to the corral gate, he stopped briefly and then began a slow curious walk to Mochaba.

The king slowly and silently slipped Mochaba a small pouch of oats and said to him quietly, "It is time for you to meet this new spirit, Mochaba. Here, make a new friend today. This young colt is why I brought you here with me; he is yours."

Tears of joy began to leak from Mochaba's eyes. With a big smile, he reached in the pouch and with an open palm gave some of those oats to the colt. He patted its right cheek and said, "You are Argento. I will care for you always, my new friend."

The king hugged Mochaba and said, "I'm proud of you, son."

They both turned and talked as they walked back to the castle.

Mochaba smiled and asked his father, "Papa, was grandfather brave?"

The king replied with much joy in his voice, "Yes, he was very brave, Mochaba. Your grandfather, King Sodamunn, was a great man of honor, a kind and respected man with a strong spirit of truth. He learned many things in his life, son, and he was fascinated with the ocean. I remember him saying to me once that even at an early age he wanted to find out where the ocean would take him. He wondered how big the ocean was and what was out there. It was his dream to explore it. When he was a young boy, about fourteen, I think, his dream was answered. He found a way to work on a ship with the English Tudor Navy, aboard the *Henry Grace à Dieu*. That ship came to port wanting to find more crew for a voyage they were manning up for, and your grandfather volunteered. The captain saw his eager interest and gave him the rank of ship's boy. That was the beginning of a new way of living for him, Mochaba. His responsibilities were to learn all he could about a large ship and its crew, but honor and bravery he learned fast. He had to. England was at war with the French. For his first six years of service, he learned deep responsibilities, and the crew learned they could count on him to follow orders. Navigation was his greatest passion, using the stars to follow a course and get to their destinations as quickly and as safely as possible. Through the years, he learned many lessons in being part of a crew on a military vessel."

King Breve saw Mochaba's interest in what he was sharing with him, and noticing a bench seat, the king said, "Let's sit down here for a minute."

Relaxed on the seat, Mochaba asked, "Did Grandfather shoot cannons?"

The king paused for a quick moment. "No, the ship had a gun crew for that, Mochaba, but I'm sure he helped keep them supplied and ready to fire when they needed to. His captain knew his leadership ability, and during the following few years, he earned his commission of masters mate and was transferred to serve on the warship, the *Mary Rose*. During his four years of service on that big ship, he made the rank he wanted, lieutenant. He was a good leader, Mochaba. He helped command the *Mary Rose* and twenty-four other vessels that patrolled the coastal shores off Europe and in the Mediterranean. In those years, son, many sea battles were fought. Some were on land too. He shared with me several battles they had to endure through his years of service. Some, he said, he would never forget. It was 1522. The second French war had started. Their ship was used to escort troops to capture the Breton Port of Morlaix. During that long tour of duty, he saw the defeat of the French army and the capture of Francis I at the battle of Pavia in 1525. The *Mary Rose* then sailed back home to Dartmouth. Your grandfather had served fourteen years with the navy and made his decision to leave the service after he had completed his contract. A few months later he fulfilled his tour of duty and asked his commander to be relieved from active duty, and it was granted. He retired his battle helmet, given to him by his captain of the *Mary Rose*, and his war saber, leaving military life behind him.

"For the next several years, he helped the harbor crews load cargo supplies on ships that came to port. I was in my young teen years when I went to the docks one morning again to see those large ships. I found a place to sit and watched him and his crew load cargo supplies on a navy vessel with many cannons. It felt good to me seeing how they all worked together. One crate after another went on board through that big vessel's two open cargo bay doors. Some of the lighter items were carried up the ship's one gangplank. I will always remember seeing your grandfather on the harbor deck just finishing up with some tie downs of a crate that needed tightening. It was on a four-wheel cart. Two men of his crew came to help him, and when it was ready, they all pushed that heavy cart through one of the cargo bays. About ten minutes later, your grandfather and the two men came back out talking together about something when he suddenly glanced over and saw me. He and those men started walking to where I was. They seemed to be in kind of a hurry. When they got to me, his friends said they would see him after their break, and then they left.

"Your grandfather was well respected at that harbor, Mochaba. The men liked him and liked the way he made decisions for action when it was needed. He said that earlier that morning a good friend of his who had served in the navy with him told him of some uninhabited land in Scotland and knew your grandfather would want to see it. I didn't know who his friend was at that time; I met him later during the early development of this kingdom. Part of his left arm had been taken in battle, and he limped as he walked. His name was Cormac. He was a very strong and intelligent man, and like your grandfather, he was a good leader, a man of justice, equality, and fairness. He said to me that your grandfather saved his life when facing a situation courageously on the battlefield, and telling your grandfather about this new land was his way of thanking him for what he had done that sad day.

"Most of the men your grandfather worked with wanted to find new land too. They all felt that building another harbor would help make better shipping for transporting products and supplies. More shipping meant steady work for them and a better living. Your grandfather shared more with me as we walked together about the changes that where going to be made. He said when they left Dartmouth they would be gone for two months, and when they returned, they would have good news for the shipping trade. Building a new kingdom was his dream, Mochaba. He wanted me to know that building a new port would lead to a new and better way of life for us."

The king smiled when he saw his son's strong desire to know more. He said, "Mochaba, your grandfather was a fair man to all people. They knew his strength and that he lived by the word of truth. That one word will never stop being the most powerful way to build trust in your life."

With a quick glance to the castle, the king said, "Mochaba, let's go see if our cooks made some of that delicious bread we both like so much. That sound good to you?"

Breve and Mochaba got up from their seats and started walking again.

Mochaba looked to his father with a proud smile and said, "I'm glad we walked together, Father."

Breve looked to his son with his smile and said, "I am too, son. There's something else that your mother and I want you to know. You're going to be part of a larger family now. Queen Siena is going to have another baby. You'll be a big brother soon. We're hoping for a girl. That would make your mother very happy. It will make me happy too. You'll be a good brother, won't you, Mochaba?"

With gladness Mochaba answered, "Yes, I will, Father. I will."

The days went by as usual for the next several months, and then finally Queen Siena gave birth to a beautiful baby girl. She loved her daughter very much. The king and Mochaba came into the master chamber where the queen was lovingly holding her newborn.

King Breve reached out to his daughter, and he showed the world a big loving smile as he gently cradled her in his arms. He said to Siena, "She's a beautiful baby, honey. I love you."

Mochaba's mother saw a big smile on her son's face too, and she said, "This is your new sister, Mochaba. Her name is Marieka."

At only five years of age, Mochaba had learned how to be responsible and a good example to others, and he kept these virtues in mind as he prepared to speak to his parents. His father was teaching him the meaning of good leadership, and Mochaba valued that always. He replied to his mother and father while showing them his respect, "I will help guide her with knowledge of our kingdom. I will protect her always."

Throughout the next fifteen years, Mochaba helped his mother and father with duties around the castle, and always he helped his sister with a little guidance as they grew up together. Marieka learned a great deal from her brother. She looked up to Mochaba. He helped her understand the value of many good virtues—being true to her word, practicing kindness, using good judgment, and having the courage to make honorable choices. Marieka remembered him saying to her that their father had taught him the importance of keeping your word—you say you will do something and then you do it; that will show good leadership and respect to the people, and they, in turn, will respect you. Their father taught them both many other values of a good leader. Being honest was most important of all.

* * *

WHEN MARIEKA WAS YOUNG, Mochaba had taught her how to saddle a horse and go riding. As she learned the skills and became confident, they would go riding together. Sometimes Marieka would challenge Mochaba to race their horses together and see just how fast they could run. Argento was never slow, and neither was Marieka's horse. Both horses ran as if they were born to compete with each other. Her horse was fast and impressive off the starting line, and once in a while, she won the competition. One day when she was fifteen, Marieka brought a friend home with her, and she asked Mochaba to go riding with them.

Something inside Mochaba made him speechless. He remembered seeing this girl before but forgot where. Even then, he had liked her. He still did, but all sorts of different, unfamiliar feelings were churning inside him. He had wanted to say hi then but had not been able to find the words. Now, here she was, Marieka's friend. All these new feelings confused him. He wanted to impress her, but for the first time in his life, he felt nervous. Quietly, he said to himself, *Okay, Mochaba, remember what Father taught you. Time to relax. Don't blow it now!*

Still nervous, he said out loud, "HI!" Suddenly his face started turning red with embarrassment.

Both girls started giggling with happy laughter.

Then Marieka said to him, "Mochaba, this is my friend Lecheenuss. She's like my big sister. She said she wanted to meet you."

The redness gradually disappeared from Mochaba's expression, and he started to relax. He felt that maybe he had been given a second chance to meet this girl. Lecheenuss walked over to him with her rosy-colored smile and said, "I'm Lecheenuss. I have seen you at my parents' market, Mochaba. I wanted to meet you when I saw you there, but I didn't know how."

Mochaba remembered now where he had seen her, and he said, "I wanted to meet you too, Lecheenuss. I wanted to say something to you, but I couldn't find the words I needed. I'm happy you're here."

They both smiled.

Then Marieka said jokingly to them, "Okay! Now that we have all that taken care of, can we go riding?"

The three of them left the castle and happily walked and talked together as they went to the stables. Lecheenuss mentioned a nice place she liked that wasn't very far away.

* * *

THE GIRLS AND MOCHABA were raised in loving families who cared for their kingdom. Lecheenuss's mother, Kylia, raised her daughter and two other children she had adopted, a boy and a girl. She was like a mother to all children because her door was always open. Lecheenuss's father, Daniel, was a fisherman. Both Kylia and he owned and managed the kingdom's marketplace. He and his crew always kept their market supplied with fresh seafood for the people. King Breve and his queen where very good friends of theirs. Queen Siena and Kylia would visit and talk together as good friends do while Marieka and Lecheenuss would play. Kylia was a very good cook, always making new recipes for her family. She was part of the charity group that the queen had organized years before in their kingdom.

The king's one brother, Herb, owned the apple orchards near town. Herb and his son, Rodolfo, always offered their help when Daniel needed it. Rodolfo worked with repairs to Daniel's fishing boats and at times offered his help in their marketplace too. The king and his family helped when it was needed. Mochaba and Marieka would often visit with their uncle and cousin to help them work their land. As Marieka got older, she would go there to learn more about the science of botany from their uncle and the other experts. They were all good friends and neighbors of the kingdom and always offered their help.

* * *

WHEN MOCHABA AND THE GIRLS made it to the stables, he asked Marieka how her new garden was going.

She said, "Oh, Mochaba, I didn't tell you, did I? I discovered a new process for growing my new plants, and I discovered a better way to roast the coffee beans we get, and the cocoa is better now too."

He replied with joy in his voice, "Coffee and cocoa? Can we bring some of that with us, Marieka? I have a coffeepot in my saddlebag. Can we, Marieka?"

A young stable hand heard Mochaba's words and, with a smile, looking to Marieka, he said to Mochaba, "I have a few cups that you can have, Mochaba. They're right here. I'll get them for you." The young man handed the cups to Marieka and said to her, "I'm Raphael. I saw you at a town meeting a while ago. I heard you talking with some people there about your new plants and that you are using a new process now for growing them."

She responded in a shy but kind way, "I'm Marieka. You were there too? I was there talking with our horticulture experts. They have been very helpful teaching me the art and science of growing plants. Do you have a garden too, Raphael?"

Showing kindness in his smile while listening to Marieka, Raphael said, "Yes, I was there, Marieka. I don't have my garden yet, but I'm working towards that. I couldn't help overhearing you mention to those people that your garden has come alive with quality herbs and plant life. Interesting. I'm learning more ways of preserving all plant life for keeping them fresh during long periods after harvest. Are you growing your own coffee plants now, Marieka?"

"No, I'm not able to grow the coffee plant here; I import the coffee beans and put them through a special process for roasting. It works pretty well. Growing the plant here, though, won't work. The climate is wrong."

She walked up to grab the horse's reins and said she wanted to know more about his studies when they returned to town later.

Raphael first smiled to Mochaba and Lecheenuss and then to Marieka and replied to her, "Okay, Marieka. I'll be here. I'd like to try your new discovery. I heard it makes a perfect brew."

With an expression of pleasant curiosity on her face, Marieka finally mounted her horse and sat comfortably in her saddle. She looked to Raphael with a smile and nodded her head yes as the three of them rode together slowly to Marieka's garden.

They didn't say much to each other. They just were enjoying the slow walk on horseback. Mochaba and Lecheenuss knew that Marieka was unusually quiet. They both saw the pleasant expression still on her face. Marieka didn't realize her happiness was so obvious. Mochaba looked to Lecheenuss, winked his left eye to her, and with a calm voice said to whoever might hear him, "I'm glad we have this time to go riding together. Aren't you, Lecheenuss?"

They got to her garden, and Marieka dismounted and walked to one of her tables to pick up the couple of small sample sacks of her coffee and cocoa. Then she walked back to her horse, put the sacks in her saddlebags, and remounted. The three rode slowly out of the kingdom for several minutes. Then, as they passed the last building of the town, the girls looked at each other, gave their horses a sudden kick, and took off at a full gallop, laughing as they started their race. They surprised Mochaba. He felt silly just sitting in his saddle watching them ride away. Faster and faster Marieka and Lecheenuss rode leaving a cloud of dust trailing behind them as their horses gained a greater speed. The girls both leaned forward to let their horses run with free determination to go faster.

Suddenly Mochaba gave Argento a kick. He reared up on his hind legs and, with a loud snort of excitement, launched into a very aggressive run before his front hooves even touched the ground. Argento ran as if he was born to race, quickly gaining greater speed, and was soon catching up to the girls. Mochaba had never seen him run so fast before. Mochaba's balance was challenged by the increasing speed his stallion had discovered. The wind force the ride created made Mochaba's eyes water, and soon he felt he could barely hold on. He tightened his handgrip, kept his heels lowered in the stirrups, and then yelled with enjoyment and excitement, "Yes, Argento, yes! You're on fire, my friend! Let's show the world how it's done! We're catching up to the girls! Ha, Argento, my friend! Ha!"

Mochaba lowered his head and chest closer to Argento's neck to help keep his balance and reduce wind drag in the surprising speed the stallion was making. They passed the girls, and Marieka yelled out with laughter, "Show off!"

He gathered in the reins, and Argento began to slow down, fell into a walk, and after a few steps, stopped and waited for the girls. With an expression of joy on his face, Mochaba was catching his breath as the girls reached him. They, too, had gradually slowed their pace from a gallop to a slow walk. The three slowly rode together, laughing in the spirit of exhilaration and companionship. A few minutes later, they came to a nice shady spot by a stream. They dismounted and loosened the saddles on their sweaty horses.

Mochaba built a fire so they all could relax for a little while. He got his coffeepot out and a few apples he had brought with him and walked the short distance to the stream where the horses were drinking. After giving them each an apple, he gently patted their sides and said to each of them, "Bless your strong spirits, my beauties."

He knelt down at the stream to fill his coffeepot and then walked back to the fire where the girls were setting out snacks. Several hours passed while they talked in easy conversation, laughed together, and shared the special coffee. Suddenly with enjoyment in her voice, Marieka stood up and asked her brother and Lecheenuss if going back home now would be okay. With a big smile to Marieka, Mochaba said, "Yes, we could do that, Marieka. I bet your new friend is waiting with anticipation to see you again. I think Raphael is a good person, Marieka. He studies horticulture. Did you know that he also studies—"

"I don't know him, but I like him," Marieka interrupted with excitement and her biggest smile. She continued talking, "Do you think he likes me? Let's save some coffee for him. Do you think he's still there? Can we go now?"

Lecheenuss looked to Mochaba with her beautiful loving eyes, and with a kind gesture and a smile, she said to Marieka, "Slow down. What really matters is how do you feel? I like people who show good manners, are kind to one another, show integrity and that they care for each other, and don't try to create friction in someone's life. Raphael seems to be like that, Marieka. I bet he's excited to see you again too."

Mochaba felt he was the luckiest person alive hearing those words from Lecheenuss. He replied also to Marieka, "Sis, always be true and honest to yourself first. Remember to think about things clearly. If you have questions, we will be here to help you. Let's go back to town now."

They all cleaned the area where they were sitting and walked to their horses to saddle up and start back home.

It was still daylight when they got back, and Raphael was in the corral shoeing one of the horses. They went into the stables and began removing all their tack. About five minutes later, Raphael came in to help. Marieka handed him the sack of coffee she had saved and asked if he would heat some water for them.

With a kind look to Marieka, Raphael smiled and said, "Yes. All of you please make yourselves at home when you finish. I'll be right back with some coffee. I'm ready for some of this delicious brew."

The three finished removing their tack, brushed their horses, and walked them to the stalls. Marieka got the three cups they had with them, picked another off one of the shelves, rinsed all, and set them on the table before they sat down. Raphael returned with the pot of coffee and filled the four cups. After he sat down with them, he asked Mochaba if he wanted to know more about the new grain he used now for the horses. Mochaba asked if it had anything to do with Argento's unusual burst of speed that day. He described how Argento had run and how surprised he was with the horse's strength and stamina, catching up with the girls' horses. Raphael said he was using a new brand of oats and some herbs he used in preparing the ground before planting now. He assured them that this new brand was much healthier for their horses than what he formerly used.

Mochaba asked, "What makes this a better feed for our horses than what we had before?"

Raphael said that this preparation added better nutritional qualities to the soil. The plants grow as a stronger crop. The animals grazing that pasture gain a better ability to sustain physical strength and even increase their intelligence.

Marieka asked if her horse was eating the same oats because she felt hers ran with better strength also.

Raphael answered, "Yes, now the feed is given to all the livestock." He asked her, "Did you notice a higher level of endurance in his run, Maricka? Maybe you saw an increased spirit of determination. The herbs I use now dominate all others. But it's not perfect yet. There's something missing, and I'm having trouble figuring out what it is."

Marieka mentioned that she also used a similar approach to growing her plants but that she too came to a point where it was difficult to find the answers she needed.

Looking to Marieka with a shyness in her expression, Mochaba added, "I know someone who can help you, Raphael. Marieka studies horticultural science all the time. Her garden has the best vegetables and fruits that she grows herself. Her studies have really done her well. She has a mastery of growing plants."

Raphael smiled while he listened to Mochaba and, with a caring glance at Marieka, said, "Thank you, Mochaba. Marieka, I would like to hear more about your teachings. Will you help build our future with me?"

Marieka had a very creative nature. She had lived her childhood years working with the kingdom's horticultural experts learning the intensive subset of agriculture that deals with many types of edible vegetation—fruits, vegetables, nuts, herbs, sprouts, seeds, seaweeds, the cocoa plant, coffee, and flowers. She loved flowers. Included in her studies were the medicinal plants and non-food crops, such as grasses.

Her shy expression left as she smiled and with a sparkle in her eyes answered, "I've always studied botany and always will. I love the values that plants give in the nutrition for life. It will be an honor and a privilege to work with you, Raphael, and I look forward to the better days ahead in learning more with you."

They finished their coffee, and Raphael smiled with joy as he stood up and said he should finish his work there now. He reached to Marieka and said that he had never met someone like her before and was very pleased to finally find the person who would help find solutions in both of their areas of interest. As he walked out to the corral, he told all three that anytime they needed him for anything to just let him know and he'd be there.

The other three got up from the table. Mochaba collected the four cups and set them up by Raphael's sink before they all started to walk home. Mochaba and Marieka walked with Lecheenuss to her house first. When they arrived, Mochaba told Lecheenuss that he was very happy they met and asked to see her again.

She replied with gladness to them both, "I had so much fun with both of you today. Marieka, thank you for asking Mochaba to be with us." With such a special, caring look in her eyes, Lecheenuss smiled to Mochaba and said to him, "I liked meeting you, Mochaba. Would tomorrow be all right with you? I'd like seeing you again too."

He looked to his sister with a thankful smile and then to Lecheenuss. His thoughts for her were so special. He felt he had just met the person he could share the rest of his life with. Mochaba said to Lecheenuss, "Yes, everyday would be good, Lecheenuss. I had a lot of fun today too. I look forward to seeing you again. I thank Marieka for us to finally meet."

Marieka smiled with such a joy in her heart hearing her brother and Lecheenuss talk together that way. She felt a happiness that she had helped them start a wonderful friendship. Marieka walked a step over to them, and without saying a word, she gave them both a brief and loving hug.

They all said their goodbyes to each other, and then Mochaba and Marieka turned and started their walk back home. They talked with each other as they walked, mainly about the wonderful day they all had.

* * *

MOCHABA AND MARIEKA sometimes went riding with their father when he could leave the kingdom for a while. The king was a wise man and a loving father. Mochaba and Marieka liked when he showed them all the land the family had earned in the days before they were born. He explained a lot to them and expressed sadness about the battles that he, his brother, and other men of Munndora had to fight against others who tried taking the kingdom away from them.

King Breve was a dream maker for his kingdom. He was a great leader of this land, always protecting his people with honor and truth whenever challenged by others, but his love for good coffee was his comfort. He called this his "meditation beverage." Every day after he blessed his kingdom to God, the queen would prepare his special brew. She was a very loving woman, supporting her husband's truth and courage and raising their two children, especially teaching her daughter the values of healthy foods. Growing foods was how Marieka lived her dream.

* * *

SEVERAL WEEKS AFTER MOCHABA, Marieka, and Lecheenuss's horse race, the king was in his castle kitchen putting some water in his coffeepot to heat and enjoy a cup of coffee. Mochaba walked in, and they both sat at the table and talked while having coffee. Mochaba asked his father for advice about a girl he liked and wanted to know better, but wanted to do it in the right way.

The king chuckled, but he understood his son.

Mochaba said he wanted to show that he cared about her, adding that she was the daughter of a good friend of his father's and he knew the family well.

The king said to his son, "Every girl loves to receive flowers, Mochaba. That's how I introduced myself to your mother, by giving her a bouquet of beautiful flowers." Things got quiet for a minute, and he said, "I know Marieka will help you pick the right flowers. She's in her garden now."

Mochaba thanked him and then scooted his chair from the table to go outside and find his sister. He walked into her garden and asked if she would help him pick the right flowers to give to Lecheenuss. He said, "Sis, I know this might seem too fast, but I feel a joy I've never felt before I met Lecheenuss. I want to give her some flowers. Will you help me, Marieka?"

Marieka said, "Lecheenuss? Boy, it's about time, Mochaba. I sure like her. I have the perfect ones she'll love. I have a vase too. Give me about thirty minutes or so. Okay?"

Mochaba walked away thinking to himself, *What did she mean, It's about time? I just met her. I do like her. Did I miss something? Is there something I'm not seeing here?*

After a short while during his walk, he was greeted by a person he thought he recognized but wasn't sure. Then he thought, *Oh, Lecheenuss's sister.* He hadn't seen her in a long while.

With a shy smile, the girl said, "Hello."

Mochaba smiled back and said, "Hi." They talked for only a few minutes, and then he asked her if Lecheenuss was home right now.

Her smile slowly disappeared, and in an aggressive manner, she said to him, "I DON'T KNOW WHERE SHE IS!" She then just quietly walked away, not saying another word.

Mochaba stood there watching her walk away and wondering to himself, *Why did she do that? I know I didn't say anything wrong. Was I too direct in asking her that? What was her name again?* He shrugged his shoulders and thought, *Oh well,* and walked back to the garden, not giving the girl's words another thought.

While he was away, Marieka had made a gorgeous flower arrangement for him. Carefully she handed Mochaba the beautifully colored vase holding the flowers and foliage.

Speechless, he held it and with both hands slowly and carefully turned the bouquet to look closer and admire the arrangement of colors. He thought to himself, *Thank you so much, Marieka.* A calm minute of silence passed, and then he said, "These are so beautiful, Marieka. What perfect colors you chose for me to give Lecheenuss. The canna lilies and foliage remind me of the soft rosy glow of her cheeks when she smiles. I know she'll love the roses—lavender, burgundy, red, and white—all with a wonderful sweet scent. Thank you so much for these flowers, sis. I owe you one."

"Sure," Marieka said. "Let's race our horses soon. Tell Lecheenuss I said hello."

Mochaba waved a thank-you to her with a free hand as he left. During his walk, the vase suddenly started to tip to one side and was about to spill out the flowers. He quickly caught it before it did.

Some of the people in town noticed that, and they all started clapping with joy and said, "Good recovery, Mochaba. Hey, when's the wedding? We want to be part of the celebration. Please send us invitations, okay?"

With embarrassment, Mochaba only smiled and nodded his head yes while thinking about what the people had said. *A wedding?* His thoughts were plenty and thoroughly clear to himself, and he felt so happy as he walked. Soon he arrived at Lecheenuss's home. Walking up to her doorway, he didn't even have to knock. Lecheenuss had been watching and opened the door before he had a chance and greeted him on the porch. Not knowing what to say, she just softly reached both hands to the proffered flower vase. Tears began to spill from her eyes as she held the most beautiful arrangement of colors she had ever seen. Slowly and carefully, Lecheenuss set the vase down on the porch and noticed Mochaba kneeling down with her.

They both looked into each other's eyes as they stood up slowly together, and with a gentle hug, Mochaba said to her, "I feel blessed to have met you, Lecheenuss. I'm happy Marieka helped this to happen. I know this might feel too fast, but inside me, I know that I love you. Anything you want or need, anything at all, you will have it. I want to share the rest of my life with you. Will you marry me, Lecheenuss? Be my queen?"

With happy tears freely watering in her eyes now and showing her cheerful rosy complexion, Lecheenuss smiled, and they embraced each other. After a loving kiss, she said, "Yes, Mochaba, yes. You are the love in my life. I will marry you."

Suddenly her mother, Kylia, came out with tears of joy for them and gave a strong loving embrace of approval. Kylia said with excitement, "Oh, I can't wait to tell your father the news. He'll be so happy. Even before you met each other, we both prayed that you two would soon be as one. Oh, I have to make a special dish. Mochaba, do you like seafood? Lecheenuss, I'll be back soon; I'm going to the market. Mochaba, tell your parents hi for me. Tell them we'll see them soon, okay? We love you, Mochaba. Bye now." She left, and as she walked to the market, Kylia gradually calmed and slowed her excited, fast steps to a relaxed walk.

Both Lecheenuss and Mochaba could tell that Kylia was so happy. Lecheenuss picked up the flower vase and carried it inside to set it on top of their family table. She asked Mochaba to have a seat as she walked into her kitchen, mentioning that Marieka had given her some of her fresh coffee grounds a couple of days ago. In the kitchen, she prepared some coffee for them and rejoined Mochaba while it brewed, saying it would take only a few minutes. The couple talked excitedly—sometimes with moments of calm—in planning their new lives together. Lecheenuss asked if they could marry under the clear sky at the special place where they had picnicked after the horse race by the stream. Mochaba said that sounded very nice to him too.

Lecheenuss got up from the table to bring their coffee. Mochaba started to stand, and just before he stood up from his chair, Lecheenuss said to him with a kind hand gesture, "Mochaba, my love, you are my king. I have honest feelings inside, and I want to practice being your queen. Please be seated. I'll be right back."

Mochaba sat back in the chair while Lecheenuss went for their coffee. When she returned and sat with him, he saw that she also brought the cocoa that he loved so much too. They both talked about their plans while they sipped the delicious new brew. They soon finished their plans, and Mochaba said he should meet with his parents and tell them the good news. They both stood, and Lecheenuss turned to him. With her loving smile, they embraced each other and kissed.

She said to him, "You are my love, you are my king. I love you."

Mochaba was so happy to have Lecheenuss in his life that he walked home with a happy skip in his steps. Finally, he arrived at the castle, and as he walked in through the main entry, he was greeted by the king's porter. Mochaba asked him where his father was and was told the king was in the throne room kitchen making some coffee. As Mochaba walked, he followed a very pleasing fragrance that filled the air. When he got to the kitchen, he saw the king pouring a cup of coffee and asked if he could join him.

While pouring a cup for Mochaba, his father said, "Let's sit at the round table."

Breve set the coffeepot back down on the wood stove, and they walked to the table to sit and talk awhile. He asked, "Did the flowers work for you, son?"

As Mochaba took his first sip, he replied with gladness in his voice, "Yes, they did, Father. Thank you. Today I asked Lecheenuss to marry me, and she said yes. Isn't that great, Father? She loves me."

This brought happiness to the king's heart. He reached his right hand over to Mochaba's left shoulder and, with a voice of respect and a brief pat to his son's back, said, "She's a beautiful person in every way. Marieka has always spoken well about her. She says Lecheenuss is her sister. We all love her, Mochaba. Congratulations. We have some planning to do now, don't we? I feel like having some chocolate with our coffee. Sound good to you, my son?"

The king and Mochaba spent the rest of the day talking and planning this celebration. Halfway through that day, Queen Siena and Lecheenuss's parents walked in and expressed how happy they all were and shared their ideas with Mochaba. Later that early evening, they all agreed to give Lecheenuss her wish and have her wedding at the location where Mochaba and she had had their first real meeting.

In the days that followed, all the people of Munndora received wedding invitations, and the following week, Mochaba and his beautiful bride were married. The people embraced her with love and celebrated with joy that evening. Mochaba and Lecheenuss soon left to begin their new life together in their new home that Uncle Herb gave them as a gift by one of his orchards.

Raphael and Marieka were so moved that evening to witness the beginning of a happy new life for Mochaba and Lecheenuss. They were both so much alike in their creative and innovative thinking. Raphael gently touched Marieka and said he wanted her to know how much he felt for her. Then he handed her a very small, decorated gift.

Taken by surprise, at first she just softly caressed it with both hands and felt a comfortable warmth in her feelings.

Looking into each other's eyes, they embraced. Then Raphael said to her, "Marieka, I miss seeing you when you go to your home each day after our studies. You said to me once that you are so happy and encouraged working with me. I love seeing that tender gleam of happiness in your eyes and your laughter of enjoyment during our days of study and research. Your smile is so pleasant to see when you finally discover a solution for all your tireless efforts."

As Raphael finished speaking, Marieka gently opened her present and saw a beautiful ring sitting in yellow-and-pink colored padding. With small tears of joy in her eyes, she touched Raphael as he knelt down before her.

Gently holding her hand and with a loving and caring voice, Raphael said, "Marieka, I will love you all my life. Will you marry me? Will you be my wife?"

Marieka helped Raphael stand so she could look into his eyes, and they embraced. With both hands, she softly touched his face and replied, "You have helped my happiness more than you know, Raphael. I need you. I feel my loneliness each day when I go to my home alone. I want to be with you always, Raphael. You are my love. Yes, I will marry you."

During the next few days, both Marieka and Raphael met with the king and queen. In utmost respect, Raphael asked them for their daughter's hand in marriage.

The wise king was a loving father to his family and to his people. With a smile of happiness he replied, "You have been like a son to us both, Raphael. Yes, your wish for our daughter's hand is given."

With blessings from the king and queen, Marieka and Raphael married soon after. Raphael became an important member of the king and queen's business with products for the kingdom. Several days after their wedding, King Breve told Raphael and Mochaba to bring their wives to the throne room the next morning and have breakfast with him and the queen.

That next morning, Mochaba and Lecheenuss walked to the castle and into the throne room. The queen was putting a few things on a silver tray for them when Raphael and Marieka also entered the room. They were all surprised to see a new table in the room near the large round table. The queen walked to the large table and set a quilted table-cloth she had made for this occasion down on the center. Then she said their coffee would be ready soon. She said for them to have a seat and walked back to her kitchen. Before they sat down, they all walked over to the new table to have a closer look. The beautiful dark-colored grain in the tabletop impressed them all. After a few minutes admiring the wood as well as the workmanship, they returned to the large table and sat down talking to each other.

Soon the queen returned to the table carrying the silver tray of items for them and set it gently down on the colorful quilt.

Lecheenuss said, "What a beautiful table you have, My Queen. Is this the rosewood that was brought to Munndora recently? My father mentioned it a few weeks ago. It's so beautiful. Is there any more of this wood?"

The queen sat down with them and replied, "Oh yes, this was from that shipment you mentioned. Mochaba's cousin Rodolfo made it for you."

Both Lecheenuss and Mochaba looked puzzled.

Lecheenuss said, "For me? You mean he made it for you, don't you, My Queen?"

"No," the queen answered. "I spoke correctly. We are all so pleased to have you as part of our family, Lecheenuss, that we have something wonderful for you and Mochaba. And, Raphael, you are also a blessing to our family. We have a surprise for you and Marieka too."

Right then the king entered carrying a tray with six cups of coffee. As he carefully set it down on the table, he gave his queen a quick kiss, sat down, and said to them all, "Good morning, my sons and daughters." He looked to his wife, and as he smiled, he said, "I like how that sounds! Don't you, My Queen?"

Breve began talking of the decision Siena and he had made shortly after the second wedding. After several minutes of talking, he got up from his seat and walked casually over to his wall cabinet. He reached in it and carefully removed two items from it, one at a time, as he spoke. He carried each to the nearby table by his family and set them down on it. They were the two items his father had given him when Breve was young: the battle helmet and the sheathed war saber. Then he walked back to his chair and sat down to have another sip of their delicious coffee. After his first sip, he said with much confidence to them all, "We both wanted to meet with all of you this morning, as your mother and father, as well as your king and queen. We are so blessed to have this family. Mochaba, your mother and I are very happy you have grown to be the man you are, showing intelligence and good leadership in your life and with the people of this kingdom. I've had meetings with representatives of our people and with others in the lands we send our supplies to. I have learned that they honor you, Mochaba. Your word is strong with them. You treat all with equal respect. They respect you very much. Your mother and I know you have learned the qualities of being a good leader and a good king. It is pleasing to know that you have what it takes to be admired by all, including your mother and me. Your grandfather would be proud of you too, Mochaba. You are ready now, my son. I give you what my father gave me. Your mother and I are so happy to say the kingdom is now yours." Breve stood up from his chair, as did the others at the table, raised both hands to Mochaba, and declared him the new king of the land.

Mochaba paused for a moment while the others all sat back down in their chairs. He felt very proud hearing those words from his father. Still standing tall, Mochaba replied, "I am honored to be given this, Father. With grandfather's battle helm of safety, Father, I will always give him honor. I do wish I had known him. I will always remember and live up to what you have taught me about him. You gave me Argento when I was young. He's a good spirit, Father, and a strong runner. I learned from you and Mother throughout the years very important lessons—to listen to the people, support them, and encourage them. I have learned from you the values of being a good leader and the meaning of being the king of this land and am pleased I have earned the respect of the people. Since I was very young, Father, you taught me that being honest was most important. Giving my word and keeping it are the important values of good leadership. You and mother have taught me many values, including keeping things simple and caring with respect for all life. Thank you, Father. Thank you both for teaching me these values I have in my life. I am proud to be in this family."

Siena got up from her chair and walked to the kitchen to bring more coffee for them. When she returned to the table, they were all talking and planning. While she started pouring their coffee, Breve spoke with enjoyment in his voice to Raphael. "Siena and I were curious of your plans, Raphael. We know that one day you and Marieka want to begin harvesting crops in greater quantity. Have you decided where you will begin planting your orchards for this?"

Raphael replied, "We both have thought about it for some time. We were told of some land several days' ride west of here located near the waterfront but heard that it had been obtained by another. We both are still looking, though. One of the crew hands from that last shipment that left Munndora a few weeks ago mentioned it to me. He also described a land far to the east of here in the waters of the Pacific Ocean. It is said the land is plentiful but not much else is known of it. He said they have passed its western coast only once on a long voyage they had for supplies needed for the land of Alkebulan. They used its shoreline from a great distance away as they passed it to help guide their ships by Nova Hollandia, but never stopped on its shores. That faraway land has us curious, and I would like to see if the conditions are as we've imagined they would be."

Breve thought for a moment with concerned feelings in his heart. Then he said, "I didn't realize that you and Marieka thought about exploring, Raphael. It is what Marieka's mother and I did before we settled here for my father. My captain spoke of this land quite some time ago to me too." Breve paused briefly for a thought and then said, "Do you know what it would take to travel that far? We have very limited knowledge of passage to that part of the world. The open seas can be very rough and very dangerous. A long journey it would be. This is interesting, though. The crew has to be very experienced. Your safety and theirs would depend on it. Raphael, have you thought this through? I mean, your safety and our daughter's safety are important to us. Have you and she considered all the conditions you would face? That type of quest on open seas delivers much to the spirit of man, and I do understand that Raphael, but our daughter. . . . It isn't that we don't, I mean, won't you reconsider this?" He paused for only a second and then said, "Raphael, Siena and I also heard about that property not far from here. Maybe it still is available. But the Pacific Ocean is a serious concern, Raphael. Give that some more thought. My wife and I will too."

Mochaba began talking with Raphael. "I too have heard about that land. Uncle Herb told me about it and said there are plenty of acres that could be developed for crops. It would be more local and better for Marieka and you to start with, I think. Maybe land near it can be purchased."

Hearing Mochaba's thoughts and listening to his father's words, Raphael agreed to the difficulty and the dangers of the longer voyage to the east and admitted his concerned feelings for him and Marieka. But he added that the supply ship that comes to Munndora every year would be willing to take them next year for a fee. Both he and Marieka agreed, though, with Breve to talk more about it.

Marieka said she thought the area her father spoke of near Munndora would be a good beginning for their plans, but the climate was her main concern. Though the new land to the east would be a difficult choice to make, it could be the correct one for Raphael and her to grow and harvest many large crops.

Breve got up from the table and walked to his desk to pick up a packet of documents he had left on it. As he walked back to the table with a smile, he handed the papers to Raphael and said, "Son, Siena and I didn't want to give these to you both right away because we wanted to surprise you. I was going to ask you and Marieka to ride with us to see something we knew you would like. Raphael, Marieka, Siena and I were the people who purchased that property you spoke of. It is our wedding gift to you both."

In a loss for words, Raphael started reading the documents. On one attached to the bill of sale, Breve had written, "To our new son and all our hopes for his success in starting his new beginning with our family. Our wish is to honor you, Raphael, as you honor us." He and Siena had signed it.

With such a joyous feeling in his heart, Raphael reached to Breve to shake hands and said, "You are truly a dream builder. Thank you."

Breve reached both arms out with a caring grasp of Raphael shoulders and said, "You are our son too, Raphael, and we want to help you. Try this land out near here first. Next year, if you still feel that you want to travel the open seas through new waters, then we'll make a plan for it. Okay, my son?"

Siena stood up from her chair and with a bright smile said, "We love all of you." As she walked to her kitchen, she said, "I'm hungry now, aren't you? Let's have some breakfast." She told her cook, "Chef

Kim, we're ready now," and within seconds, three servers came in and began serving.

They all enjoyed their morning breakfast together and talked more of how they all would help support each other in their new lives. They continued talking together about planning to go to the new property too. When they finally finished their breakfast, they all left the castle and walked while talking more together about their plans for the days ahead. In a short time, each of them started going to a separate location to attend to his or her responsibilities for the day. Marieka went to her garden in town and thought about the things she and Raphael had talked about with her father. The others were equally busy throughout that day.

Later that evening at the castle, Breve thought to himself how pleased he was that the day had turned out so well. But still he felt troubled about the distant land Raphael had mentioned. Breve entered the throne room and decided to sit and relax for a little while before recording the events and decisions of the day. Just before closing his eyes to rest, he noticed some papers on the large table near him and assumed Siena had left them and was taking a break for a minute.

About a half hour later, Siena walked in and saw Breve relaxing. She walked quietly to the kitchen, and as she passed by him, he opened his eyes and gave her a big smile. Still walking, she asked if he would like some fresh coffee. He agreed with her, and after a couple of minutes, he stood up, went to the bookshelves to get the current record book, and took it to his roll-top desk. Picking up his writing quill, he added his updated notes.

Several minutes had passed when Siena walked back in with two cups of their favorite coffee. She stopped briefly at the large round table where her papers were sitting, placed her cup down by them, and then walked to Breve's desk and set his cup down quietly.

Breve said to her as she turned and walked back to the table, "Thank you, my queen. I love you."

She turned her head back to him as she walked, and with a big glowing smile, she replied with a soft whisper, "I love you too, sweetheart. I'll be over here." She sat and worked on her papers.

Twenty minutes went by when Breve again suddenly remembered something about the new land in the Pacific Ocean that Raphael had mentioned. It brought back many fond memories of his early years. While he paged through his record book, he read and evaluated some of the accomplishments and thrills he and Siena had lived through. It also reminded him of some other things he tried so hard to forget—about protecting his people in battles against others who had tried stealing his kingdom's rights to live free. He remembered the day his father, King Sodamunn, told him of times when he had traded with the local natives and when trouble came to this land the natives themselves also helped the king fight his enemies. King Sodamunn instilled in Breve's heart the importance of giving respect to all life, knowing when to be kind, and earning the respect of others by being a man of your word.

Breve couldn't help but feel some sadness about their daughter and Raphael's thoughts of going to a new land far away, but he knew his daughter's heart and courage. The adventure of discovery was still strong in his blood too. He understood Raphael having that interest in a new land, but now he knew the property he and Siena had given them was something they had wanted and would build on.

He finished writing his notes and got up from his seat to place his book back on the shelf.

Siena noticed that her husband was unusually quiet and tired. She stood up and walked over to him showing her loving and caring smile, wrapped both arms around him, and hugged him tightly. Gently placing both hands around his face, Siena looked deeply into his tired eyes and said softly with a caring voice, "Honey, I know you are thinking of some things that are distant from our lives right now. I'm so happy that my love for you is what I live for always. You are my king, and I am proud of you, my husband. Let's talk awhile before we go to that place in our dreams, we know so well. I'll bring us some fresh fruit that I brought yesterday."

As Breve sat down, Siena went to the kitchen and prepared a tray of some nourishment for them both. When she returned, she placed the tray by her husband and sat down beside him.

Breve said with a glad expression in his voice, "I'm so happy you are with me, Siena. You are my treasure in life. I know Marieka and Raphael may want more land, but I feel as you do. My life has always been wonderful knowing you were with me. That property we gave them, I think I'd like to live near there, wouldn't you? It was said to me there's more land there, so I had some men go with supplies to start the development of our daughter's property and to look at that land around theirs. I could get Herb and a few of my men to go there with me and have a close look at that land. Does that sound all right with you, Siena?"

Siena said, "Yes, I'd like that. I'd like to know something, though. Will you be okay moving from Munndora?"

"Yes, I would like to build a new place for us. When Raphael mentioned that new land far from us, I did feel a bit worried about it, but it reminded me of the joyful times we shared in discovering new places. Our daughter and Raphael are smart thinkers. They want to explore just as we did. It made me curious, and since our son is starting his new life as king, I thought giving him room to make his decisions would be the best thing for him. I think Herb will want to go there with me. The weather is good now. Riding there on horseback, though? I think I'd rather go by sea. We could take the *Cutter*. It's our smaller ship, and it's been docked a few days. I know it has most of the supplies onboard that we'll need. Yes, I want to take a good look at that land again, Siena. I'll see the harbor captain about using the ship for a couple of weeks. What do you say, hon? If we left tomorrow, we'd be back in two weeks."

Siena answered, "Yes, I like that idea. Going to a new location with you, even to a place that is just a short distance, makes me happy. What is important to me is we are together. Thinking of the adventures that we've shared together makes me feel so happy. I will always remember when we went through the waters of the Mediterranean and walked on the shores of Sicily. Oh, I love you so, Breve. I loved it when you and I walked through the Cappella Palatina. I'll always remember that part of our lives." Showing her delightful smile, she said, "God is beautiful."

"Yes, he is, sweetheart. I'm glad we were there too."

Feeling a bit tired, Breve smiled and said, "Hon, I'm sleepy. How about you?"

"Yes, I'm feeling tired too. Let's get some rest."

Breve helped his wife organize her papers and clean the table before they walked to their chambers and climbed into bed. Soon they both fell into a deep sleep.

The next morning, Breve was awakened by a delicious aroma in the air. Siena was already awake, but she wasn't in the chambers. He got up and dressed thinking, *Mmmm, that smells so good. But where is Siena?* He followed the aroma to the main kitchen and saw his wife.

Siena was just then pouring a delicious-looking sauce in one of the small bowls. She said, "Good morning, handsome."

"Good morning, my love," he answered back. "What are you cooking, Siena? It smells good, whatever it is."

"It's a recipe Kylia gave me a few days ago, and I decided to use it to cook something for you myself this morning. It does smell good, doesn't it?"

"Yes, it does. Yes, it does."

Siena put the stirring spoon down on the counter and reached for her hot pads so she could remove something from the hot brick oven. With both hands, she carefully slid out a tray of bread rolls that she had baked and proudly walked it slowly past Breve. As he inhaled deeply with a smile, she said, "I know you love fresh-baked breads, honey. Mmm, these do smell heavenly delicious, don't they? Wait till you taste the new gravy recipe I prepared for you."

Breve followed the intoxicating scent as if it had control of his every step to the table, smiling and softly inhaling deeply as Siena slowly placed the tray down in the center of the table on top of a beautiful colored quilted pad she had made. Still smiling with his eyes barely open, he sat down in his chair.

Siena said, "I'll get our coffee and the other items for us. Only take a second, hon."

Breve volunteered to help her, but she said not to bother. So he just waited in his seat with a child-like smile in anticipation of the meal to come.

She returned with the last item and said, "I love you, sweetheart. Let's give our thanks before we eat." She sat down and reached to his hand.

They bowed their heads and payed homage, "Thank you for our lives, Father. Guide us all safely through this day."

Breve then reached to the roll basket and offered the first one to his wife. She then reached to the gravy bowl and said, "Oh, I think you're going to like this, hon."

They soon finished their morning breakfast.

Breve helped his wife clean the kitchen and dry the plates. He said, "You know, Siena, I kind of like doing things by ourselves again, don't you? It helps me remember all our days together."

Siena smiled and with a loving expression in her eyes, she reached her arms around her husband and said softly, "Breve, I'm so happy with our lives together. The memories of my life with you have always made me feel so warm and comfortable inside. I feel so blessed knowing you are my husband. I love you."

Before they stopped their hug Breve said, "You are with me, I am a lucky man having you in my life, Siena. Are you seeing Marieka today?"

They started walking from the kitchen, and she replied, "I'll see her for part of the day today. She mentioned that she wanted to show me the new plants she and Raphael planted."

Breve smiled and said, "That sounds like fun. Marieka and Raphael have learned so much together about horticulture, haven't they? I'm looking forward to having a closer look at that land near theirs. I'll be away for part of the day, Siena, a few hours I think. I'll go see the captain first and then go to Herb's. Tell Marieka hi for me and that I'd like to talk with her and Raphael when we come back to shore."

Siena replied, "I'll tell her, and I know they'll be happy to hear what you want to talk about with them."

Breve put on his cape, and they both walked to the entrance hall. Siena stopped at the doorway and said, "I hope Herb agrees to go with you."

Breve smiled and said, "I know he'll be okay with it. I'll tell him you said hi. You have a good day. Oh, let's keep this a secret between us for now, okay, sweetheart? See you tonight."

With loving thoughts of their decision, they both started their day with feelings of joy.

* * *

Siena walked back into her bedchamber and started getting herself ready to spend the day with Marieka. She had much to discuss with her. She thought she would also help pick some grapes that Marieka had mentioned—and the pineberry strawberry plants sounded delicious too.

Finally ready, Siena left the castle and walked the short distance to Marieka's garden. When she got there, Marieka opened the gate and they hugged each other.

With a smile Marieka said, "Hello, Mother. I'm so happy you came to see me. Are you ready to pick some of those new berries I have? The fruits and berries have turned out so perfect, Mother. I'll get my garden helper now, and then you and I can go to the field, okay?" She gave her mother a chair and a small basket that had a variety of her new berries for her to enjoy and said, "I know you'll like these, Mother. I'll only be a minute. Be right back." Then she walked to her storage room to get her helper.

Siena sat down and began to sample the berries. Soon she thought to herself, *Oh, these berries are so delicious.*

In a few minutes, Marieka returned with her helper and said to her mother, "This is Jana, my new helper. She studies medicine, and she has taught me a lot about the medical benefits and culinary nutrition for good body health."

With a warm smile, Jana bowed to Siena and said good morning to her.

Siena stood up from her chair, gave Jana a warm hug, and said, "Marieka said she has wonderful people who work with her. I'm so happy to meet you, Jana. Your interest is medicine? I have interest in that too. Will you be practicing this for our people soon?"

Jana felt so good hearing the words from Siena and knowing she really cared and wanted to talk with her. Jana said, "Yes, but right now, I go to the people when they need me to help them feel better."

Siena thought for a moment and said, "There will be some changes pretty soon that might affect you—but in a good way. I look forward to talking with you more."

With a shy expression Jana said, "Yes, I would like to talk with you again."

Marieka's horse was already hitched to her small wagon. She and Siena stepped up on it and sat down for the ride to the orchard. Before leaving, Marieka said to Jana, "Thank you so much for your help. We'll be away for several hours. I think you have all those other supplies for the two families I mentioned to you earlier. We'll be back before dark. See you then, Jana."

Mother and daughter left the garden talking about family doings and what Raphael had spoken of earlier. They were happy to spend the day just being together and picking berries. Marieka mentioned her discovery in growing her new strawberries.

"See these, Mother. They've all turned out so well. These new ones aren't quite ready to pick yet, though."

Marieka explained what she added to the soil, what she called "sandy loam" and a little of her special salts, to help make the strawberries deliciously sweeter and juicier. Her mother asked her if that process was how she grew all her fruits. Marieka said they were all similar but the amount of her formula was different for each different crop and the recipes required adding some of her new herbs to some of the other crops she raised. "Mother, I'm sure the berries over there are ready. Let's go see how they're doing."

They started walking the short distance talking together.

Marieka's knowledge about nutrition and healthy foods impressed Siena. She was pleased with the young intelligent woman her daughter had grown to be and so proud of her accomplishments.

Siena walked up close to her daughter and gave Marieka a hug saying, "I am so proud of you, Marieka. You have learned and know so much. Your brother said once to your father and me that he was so happy you were his sister. We are all thankful that you are the person you are. I love you, sweetheart."

They spent most of the day sharing their thoughts, pruning some of the plants, and picking the fresh fruits to fill their baskets. Before long, the afternoon began to chill, and they began to organize their pickings on the wagon. Before they rode back to town, Marieka walked up to her mother, embraced her with a hug, and said, "I love you so much. Now that Mochaba will be king, where will you and Father go? I have an idea. Would you and Father like to live with us while we cultivate our land?"

Siena said, "Why don't you bring Raphael with you after your father comes back to Munndora? He's going to be away for a short while. We can all talk about it when he gets back."

Marieka asked, "How long will he be gone, Mother? Where is he going?"

Because of their secret, Siena felt unsure how to answer Marieka's question. Hesitant for to answer, she just smiled and said, "It's nothing really, Marieka. Your father and Herb have some business away from home to finalize and will be back in two weeks."

While they rode back, they talked more about how it would be to build the new orchards and all continue with their new lives.

At the garden, Jana helped them unload the several baskets they had filled. Then she unhitched Marieka's horse from the wagon and walked him to the stables. Marieka handed her mother a small basket of some berries and nuts to take home with her and asked when she and Raphael should be at the castle. Siena said any time would be fine. Siena set the basket down and gave Marieka a loving hug, and they said their goodbyes as her mother left.

Jana returned from the stables and helped Marieka sort out the new supplies and store them to be ready for the following day. Before the sun began to set on the horizon, they caught up with all they needed to do before closing. Then Marieka handed Jana a basket of fresh berries, saying thank you for helping and she would see her in the morning. Marieka finished a few more tasks before closing her garden gate and walking home, thinking about how happy she was for having Jana as a good friend and helper. She felt a bit tired while walking home but also optimistic that something good was about to happen for her and Raphael. When she got home Raphael was just finishing one of his house hold chores for their ceiling. Marieka saw he had made something for their supper and she could help him with a ladder he was putting away, and she did. They both sat down to eat for a moment and talked together about how their day was before going to their bedroom for the night. Marieka mentioned that her mother had invited them to the castle for a meeting her father wanted to have with them.

Raphael replied, "I'd like that, Marieka. I'm looking forward to seeing them again. Did she say something about our new property?"

Marieka answered, "No, nothing about that, but when I asked for them to live with us, mother said we could come over and talk about it for a while.

Meanwhile, Siena was home. Right away, she asked one of their porters to start a fire in the fireplace. She wasn't cold; she just wanted to sit by a comfortable fire that evening. She then walked to her bedchamber to remove the dirty clothing she wore that day and put on something more comfortable to relax in. When she was ready, she walked back to the main living area and sat, enjoying the warmth of the fireplace. Siena picked up on the side table the crocheting she had been working on. She was always thankful to the lady she had befriended during her youth who had taught her crocheting and quilting.

Knowing she'd like to have a little something to eat before she started, she got up and went to her kitchen for a tray of some fruit, cheese, and a few vegetables to have by the fire. She carried the tray to her rocker and sat down with it resting on her lap. While she picked the selection of berries she liked, Siena began thinking of some beautiful times she and Breve had lived through, places they had traveled to, and things they had enjoyed doing together. She smiled and then giggled when she remembered something he had said to her when they were young. Soon the tray was bare. She took it to her kitchen, rinsed it, put it on one of the shelves, and returned to her chair.

Relaxing for a few minutes, Siena closed her eyes and thought of that new property her husband and Herb were going to see and prayed they would be safe while they were away and find it to be the perfect place for her and Breve to live. She whispered, "Please see my family safe on this venture, Father. Help keep them strong and guide their path through the days they are away."

Comfortably knowing that everything would be all right, Siena opened her eyes and reached to her creation. In a short while, she was humming and rocking in her chair. She thought of what Marieka had asked her earlier and smiled when she realized what sort of thoughts her own mother must have had when she and Breve were ready to move and live their lives together. Siena's fondest memories were those any woman enjoys—knowing she's with the man she loves and who loves her in return.

Two hours had passed, and she was close to the last row of her crocheting. She felt confident the colors she used for the pattern were perfect. Finally, it was finished. She cut the extra wool off and placed the two hooks and remaining wool on the table. Then she stood from her chair and held her work up to look at it. She said to herself, *This is the perfect gift for Marieka.*

While Siena was still holding her new creation up, Breve walked in and said, "Hi, sweetheart. Herb sends you his greetings." He noticed

Siena's new creation and walked closer to have a better look at it. He said, "Is this the one you started last week? It turned out so nice, Siena." With his right hand he touched it and said, "I like the colors you chose. It looks so warm."

Siena lowered it a little and said, "Do you really like it? I made it for Marieka. She mentioned to me that she needed a new shawl. I hope she likes it."

"Oh yes, Siena, I'm sure she will. You are so creative. I can see where Marieka gets her talents. How is Marieka? Did you both have fun today?"

She smiled with her answer, "Yes, it was such a wonderful day being with her. Our daughter has learned a lot. She said Raphael showed her a better way of preparing the ground before planting vegetables. I'm so happy for them both."

Siena put her crochet items away and walked towards the kitchen. But she stopped a second and said to Breve, "I'm so glad you're home. You must be hungry. I'll bring you a tray of what we picked today. I saved the new strawberries for you. They're delicious. I'll bring you some water too."

"Yes, that does sound good."

Siena walked to the kitchen and started preparing his tray while Breve sat at his desk to write down the day's accomplishments. When he finished, he sat back and reviewed his papers for a moment. Satisfied with what he had written, he got up from his chair and walked to the round table. Just as he sat in his chair, Siena came back in carrying the tray of assortments.

She placed it down on the table and said, "I think you'll like these. Oh, I forgot your water. I'll be right back." She quickly walked back to the kitchen and returned carrying a cup of water and set it down near the tray.

With a loving smile, Breve said, "Thank you."

Siena sat down by him and asked how his day was. With slight disappointment, Breve said, "Well, we won't be able to take the *Cutter*. It's been docked for maintenance and won't be ready to leave port for a couple of weeks. Bad rudder and needs new sails. The other two vessels we have are shipping supplies to locations other than where we're headed, so it looks like it's going to be a ride on horseback. She-ew, I can feel those saddle sores already." Breve got up and walked, simulating hurt buttocks. Then suddenly he stood up straight and laughed for a second, shaking his head a little.

Siena replied, "Oh, that does sound difficult. Could you change the time for going there, Breve? Does it have to be tomorrow?"

"Well, earlier today, we loaded our supplies on the wagon we're taking with us. Only a couple more items tomorrow, and then we'll be ready to go, so I'd rather not delay. It shouldn't be too bad for us." Breve gave her a wink of confidence with a loving smile and said, "We'll do okay, hon."

Siena smiled back with love for her husband, and the two talked and laughed while they shared their thoughts of the plans they'd started.

Several minutes passed during their conversation when Breve said, "Herb said he's glad to go and see that property with me. He'll be here tomorrow morning. We stopped by the market for some supplies today too, and Kylia said to say hello to you."

Siena asked, "Does she want me to come by there tomorrow?"

Breve answered, "She didn't say, but I'm sure she'd be happy to see you."

"Okay, yes, I'll go there tomorrow."

Breve picked another berry and said, "A few of my men are going with us too. We'll be on our way by midday."

They both felt the new plans were right for them and decided it was time for a restful night of sleep. Siena got up, carried the empty tray to the kitchen, and spent a few minutes cleaning.

Breve walked to the fireplace to examine how hot the ashes were. He grabbed the fire poker and carefully nudged some ashes to one side and then stirred them for a couple of minutes. Seeing it was safe to leave it that way and it would cool down soon, he placed the poker back with the other tools and went back to his desk to organize and put away his papers. Siena came back in as he closed the roll-top of his desk. She gave him a quick kiss, and together they walked to their bedchamber.

The next morning's sunrise peeked above the horizon east of Munndora. The pleasant cool morning air gave the new day a fresh beginning. Breve opened his eyes and saw that Siena was still asleep. Knowing that his brother would be there soon, he quietly got out of bed, dressed, and then walked to his closet and put a few clothing items in a carrying case.

Siena opened her eyes and smiled when she saw Breve preparing for the trip. The thought of what her husband was going to do for them made her happy. She sat up, rubbed her eyes, and said, "Good morning."

Breve stopped what he was doing and looked over to her with a big smile and replied, "Good morning to you, too. Did you sleep well?"

"Oh yes, wonderfully. I dreamed about us, and I loved it." Siena climbed out of bed and started getting ready for her day.

Breve smiled again and said, "We must have had the same dream. I'm so happy you're with me about this idea, Siena."

She smiled, "I'm happy too."

Breve put the last item in his case, closed it, put a strap around it, and cinched it tight. He looked over to Siena and said, "Herb should be here pretty soon."

Putting the last item of clothing on, Siena said, "I'll freshen up and then make some coffee. Oh, I forgot to mention, we're low on pumice. Is there more ground for us?"

"Oh, yes, one of our porters yesterday put some in our washroom. I think it's by the new linen we got the other day."

She smiled and said, "Thank you, honey. I'll have our coffee ready soon. Are you going to the entrance hall now?"

Breve picked up his case. "Yes, Herb should be here any minute now, I think. We'll be back for that coffee." He turned and carried his case to the entrance. When he got there, he saw the first footman open the door to let Herb in. Herb was carrying a small box of apples, which he set down by the door.

Breve set his case down by it and said, "Do you have everything ready to go, Herb? You brought your tinderbox with you, didn't you?"

"Yes, all set." Herb reached into the box and gave one of the apples to Breve and said, "Here, my brother, have one. Rodolfo picked these yesterday for us."

Breve took a bite. "Mmm, thank you, Herb."

Herb smiled and said, "I knew you'd like it and thought Siena would like some too."

Breve took another bite and said, "Wonderful. Yes, I know she'll like these, Herb."

Herb smiled as he watched Breve's expression of delight in having another bite of apple. He said to Breve. "I double-checked our supplies with the other men going with us, and everything's ready. The men are checking the last of their few supplies they're taking too. Eli, our wagon driver, said the wagon will be ready to go within the hour."

One of Siena's maids came to the entrance hall and said Siena had their coffee ready. Breve got one of his porters to carry the box of apples to Siena's kitchen for him while he and Herb followed and talked together discussing their plans for the trip.

As Siena was exiting the kitchen with the fresh coffee, the porter walked in with the box. She said as she passed him, "Oh, thank you. Place it on the kitchen counter for me, please."

When Siena returned to the kitchen, she saw what was in the box and smiled. She cut a few and placed them into a bowl to bring to the table. Breve and Herb walked in still discussing ideas for the property. Siena carried the bowl of apples, placed it on the table, and then poured their coffee.

Herb said to her as he sat down, "Thank you, Siena. It is good seeing you again."

Siena answered, "Thank you, Herb," and, when she finished pouring, sat down with them. She picked one of the apple pieces from the bowl and took a bite. "Mmm."

Herb and Breve paused in their conversation to sip their coffee.

Siena asked, "Are these the new angel apples Rodolfo told Marieka about? She said the one he gave her wasn't quite ripe yet but still was so delicious."

Herb smiled when he saw her pleasant reaction to the taste. He answered, "Yes, those are the angels. Rodolfo discovered a new and better way for intensifying the delightful taste. He picked these for us yesterday and wanted you to have some too."

"That's very nice of him, Herb. I'll thank him when I see him again."

Herb replied, "I'm pretty sure he'll be at the market helping Daniel and Kylia tomorrow."

They spent the next hour in pleasant conversation, discussing their ideas for the property and plans for the days ahead. They all were optimistic about the land Breve wanted to see and had some ideas for having a new home for Siena and Breve, but nothing would be final till Breve saw the land. They finalized their ideas and decided it was time to start their day.

Herb got up from his seat and said, "It was good talking with you, Siena. I'll help Breve with that land decision and see you when we come back."

Siena smiled and replied, "Thank you. It was good talking with you too, Herb. Be safe."

Before Herb left the room, he said, "I'll get your case, Breve, and put it on the wagon and secure it down tight for you. Everything else should be ready to go by now."

Breve replied, "Okay, Herb, thank you. I'll be only a couple of minutes behind you."

Herb walked out of the room.

Breve stayed a few minutes to finish his coffee, then got up from his chair, and helped Siena clear the table. Then he walked to his desk and collected some documents to take with him. Siena had finished putting the last few things away in her kitchen and put some bread and dried beef in a bag for Breve and his men to take on the journey before she joined him in walking to the entrance hall. When they got there, Brave hugged his wife and said, "I remember finding our paths together when we first met, Siena. Living together, I have always felt love for you. I love you, Siena."

Showing him a loving smile, she replied, "I love my life with you, my husband. You are my life. You are my king. Please be safe while you are away. You both please be safe and come home soon."

They kissed, and then Breve went outside, enjoying a refreshing morning breeze while he walked to the stables. Siena stayed in the castle and organized some chores for her servants before she went to the marketplace to visit with Kylia.

Within minutes, Breve saw Herb, the wagon driver, Eli, and the two men going with them—Lieutenant Vincent and Corpsman Marcus—securing some things on the wagon they were taking. They all spent the next few minutes double-checking everything onboard and found they had what was needed while Eli secured the tie downs for the cover of the wagon before driving it away. Herb, Breve, and the other men walked over to their horses, mounted up, and at a steady walk, rode out of Munndora and were on their way.

Back at the castle, Siena's chambermaid was cleaning the bedchamber while Siena went to her washroom to see what supplies needed replenishing at the market later. While making a list of items she needed, her daughter walked in. Siena greeted her with a smile and said, "Good morning, Marieka."

"Good morning, Mother," Marieka said with a big smile. "Rodolfo came by our house earlier and asked Raphael if he would help him in the apple orchard for a couple of hours, so I thought I'd come by for a visit before going to my garden."

Siena was pleased Marieka had come by and asked, "Would you like to walk with me to the market before you go there, Marieka?"

"Yes, I would, Mother. I need to pick up a few things too."

Siena finished her list and said, "Okay, Marieka, let me get my hat, and we'll go now."

They left the castle and walked together sharing thoughts about what they wanted their day to be like. Marieka said she and Raphael could come over and stay the night with her, if that would be all right.

Siena replied, "That would be nice. I'll make something for our supper. I think your brother and Lecheenuss will be coming by later too."

At the market, once Marieka found what she needed, she said, "Okay, Mother, I'm done here. What time should we come over today?"

"Any time would be okay, sweetheart. I'll be there after I visit with Kylia a little while and stop by the charity building."

"Would four be too early?"

"No, that would okay. I'll be home by then."

"Okay, Mother, we'll see you then. Please tell Kylia hi for me."

Siena finished purchasing the few items she needed. After looking around and not finding Kylia or Daniel, she left the market and returned to the castle to drop off the new items she got before going to the charity building. She wanted to check the food supply and see if her helpers there needed anything. When she got there, she saw there were new clothing, blankets, and shoes, as well as fresh bread. That encouraged her, and she thought about the good care the people of Munndora were giving to each other. She talked with the two people working there, and one said a man and a woman had visited last week, wanting to donate items. They said they would bring some blankets and clothing every few months. Siena asked who they were. The two workers said they had never seen them before last week. Siena was so pleased to hear there were people who cared for others as she and Kylia did. She said to tell the couple that she wanted to meet with them to arrange a program for the people who donate items.

Siena left the building feeling so happy about what she had seen. On her way home, she tried guessing who those two care-giving people could be, but she just didn't know. After a little while, she felt it didn't matter who they were; what mattered was there are other people who do care and want to help others get on their feet and stand strong with dignity, no matter who they are.

She decided to stop by the market again before returning home and see if Kylia was there. Finding Kylia helping her husband and a few others load shelves with some new produce, Siena walked over and offered to help. She removed her jacket and hat, put them on a nearby cabinet, and for the next twenty minutes till the wagon was empty, helped carry small boxes of the produce from the wagon to the shelves. Then Kylia asked if she could stay a little while and help unwrap some boxes. Siena agreed, and when they finished, they both walked to the back room where Daniel and a couple of his workers were finishing repairs to the fish nets they had used earlier that day. Then Rodolfo walked in and said hello to Siena.

Siena replied, "Hi, Rodolfo. Thank you for the apples. Are you help-ing repair the net? I want to ask you something when you finish today."

"Yes, I'm helping to carry this net to the boat. I'll be right back." And he helped the other men carry the net outside.

Kylia got up and, as she got two empty cups, said, "I have some-thing for you to try—some delicious juice I made this morning, I think you'll like it." She set the cups down on the table and then walked to a larger table where she had a cold-water container. Reaching in it, she removed a jar of liquid. "Ah yes, still chilled," she said and dried the water off the jar as she carried it to their table. Kylia opened the jar, poured a cup, and handed it to Siena, saying, "Daniel really likes this flavor. It's a sweet fruit called mango that came with our last shipment."

"Thank you, Kylia."

Kylia then poured the second cup, set it and the jar on the table by them, and sat down. "Yes, I'm happy you came to visit. I get so busy at times."

The two women drank quietly for a few moments, obviously enjoying the juice.

Kylia said, "This flavor helps me feel good. What do you think, Siena?"

Siena agreed and took another drink.

Kylia said, "Oh, your cup is empty. You must be thirsty. Here, I have more." She filled both their cups and asked if Breve and Herb had left to see the new property.

"Yes, they left this morning. Breve said they might be away two weeks, but I hope only one."

Kylia replied, "I do too, Siena. Are you okay? I mean will you be all right while he's away?"

With a slight hesitation, she said, "Oh yes, Kylia, I'm okay. I just hope they're safe and come back soon."

"I know what you mean, Siena. Sometimes when Daniel is away, I begin to feel different. I know he's all right, but I do miss him when he's out fishing and away from home for a couple of days at a time. I'm so happy when he's back home safe. He brings the love he has for me, and he knows I'm happy in love with him too."

Quietly they just sipped the delicious juice when suddenly Kylia started giggling. Siena glanced at her for a second and smiled. Another second passed, and Siena felt a sudden happiness in her thoughts. She didn't know or understand it; she just felt the joy in being there with her friend and being happy. Siena looked at Kylia's funny expression, and at that instant they both started laughing hard and loud together. Siena pointed to Kylia, and her eyes began to water, she was so happy. Not saying anything, they just both laughed harder.

Rodolfo came back in the room and asked, "What's so funny?"

The two women had no explanation. Kylia just liked to laugh and be happy and tried to explain, but she just ended up laughing more. Finally, between her breaths and trying real hard to control herself, she said, "Some . . . sometimes . . . it's better to . . . to laugh and feel young and alive."

When Rodolfo saw the happiness and expressions on their faces, he began to laugh too. For several minutes the back room was a place full of laughter. Soon, it began to get back to a more calming, quieter place, although Kylia still had an occasional giggle between her breaths while wiping happy tears from her eyes.

Siena smiled and said, "I haven't laughed like that in a long time, Kylia. It felt so good to be young like that again. Thank you, my friend."

With a big smile, Kylia said, "I'm so happy you came to visit with us, Siena. Somehow, I knew you wanted to laugh with me. If there's anything that we can do for you while Breve is away, please let me know."

Siena smiled brightly and said, "Thank you, Kylia. I do have a question. Marieka and Raphael are coming over tonight for supper, and I want to cook something for them. They both like seafood. Do you have a good salmon recipe?"

Kylia got up and walked to her desk to find her favorite, the planked–paleo pecan salmon fillet. "This is one of my favorites. Prepare it with a side of white rice and peas. Mmm, it is so good. I know you will like it. Daniel and his crew brought fresh salmon earlier this morning, and we have new spices you might like too."

Now in a calm manner, Siena said, "Thank you, Kylia. I'll have a look." She turned her attention to Rodolfo for a moment and asked, "Would you like to have supper with us, Rodolfo? I'll make enough if you'll carry the salmon home for me. I know Marieka and Raphael would be glad to see you, and they'll be there in a few hours. Mochaba and Lecheenuss may come by too."

Rodolfo smiled and answered, "I can do that," and got a box to carry them.

Siena then looked to Kylia again and said, "I had a wonderful visit, Kylia. Please say hi to Daniel for me, and let's do this again sometime."

Respecting her best friend's new position, Kylia answered, "I had fun too, My Queen. I'll tell him for you. Please also say hello to the family for us."

Siena answered, "I will do that, my friend."

Right then Rodolfo returned with the box, and he and Siena said their goodbyes and started their shopping. After finding what Siena needed, they left the market and walked to the castle. When they arrived, Siena had one of her servants carry the box to her kitchen.

Rodolfo said, "I'll go home and change and be back in a couple of hours."

Siena walked to her bedchamber to find something different to wear before cooking supper. She saw her clothing had been cleaned, folded, and placed on a freshly made bed. Such a pleasant scent in her chamber, she thought. Her room smelled so fresh. She knew her chambermaid took good care of her things. She put her clothing in her closet and then found what she had worn when she and Marieka had been in the orchard. She thought to herself, *This is what I'll wear*, and changed her clothes.

Then Siena went directly to the kitchen and started preparing the evening's supper. Before long, the prep work was done, and everything was put on three trays and covered. Two of her servants came to help and set the round table for her. Siena thanked them and said she wanted them to put fresh linens on the bed in the spare bedchamber for her daughter, and when they finished, they could have the rest of the evening to themselves.

They asked permission to come back after they prepared the room; they would be happy to help serve the meal and clean the kitchen for her when everyone finished eating.

With a surprised look and a smile, Siena answered, "Well yes, that would be nice of you. Thank you. The food will be ready to serve soon, and there is enough for both of you. I'll have my son bring the other table in the room for you."

They both replied in kindness, "Thank you. The room will be ready."

Siena gave them a cheerful smile of thanks.

After adding the last ingredient in the sauce, Siena decided to relax and have a cup of coffee with a dash of cinnamon. She put a pot of water on her stove to boil and got some documents to read for a few moments. When she heard the water boiling, she made her favorite coffee drink.

Returning back to her documents, Siena sat down and started thinking of one particular paragraph she had just read. It reminded her of how happy she and Breve had felt when they had started living their lives together. This caused her to smile with thoughts of the places they had traveled to, the people they'd met, and the family they had. The new life she and her husband were about to start, the different things they would experience together, and the idea of a new adventure together brought real joy and excitement to Siena. She felt such happiness living with Breve.

After a short while, she finished her cup of coffee and got up to make another cup. As she walked to the kitchen, Lecheenuss and Mochaba walked in the room. They noticed the table setting and asked if she had company. Siena answered with a smile, "Hi, Mochaba. Hi, Lecheenuss. Yes, this is for you. I'm making supper for us; the others will be here soon."

Mochaba and Lecheenuss didn't quite know what to say, so as they removed their jackets, they asked if they could do something to help.

Siena answered, "Oh, yes, Mochaba, would you gather more wood for the stove? There's more by the fireplace. Lecheenuss, please come help me in the kitchen."

They both eagerly did what was asked.

In the kitchen, Lecheenuss watched Siena put an empty skillet on the stove and then put some bay leaves in it. Siena said, "Here, Lecheenuss, this doesn't take but a few minutes. When you start to smell the aroma, they're done. Don't let them burn. I'll get the coriander and cumin seeds ready for you, and after each are toasted and cooled, we'll grind them together with some peppercorns. I'll get the mortar and pestle ready for us."

Lecheenuss said, "I'd be happy to do that, Siena."

Siena got one of the trays and started to cut salmon fillets.

Mochaba brought in a small box of wood and placed it near the stove. Then he got a cup to make himself some coffee.

"Thank you, Mochaba. Two of my servants will be here soon to help me with our supper. I invited them to have supper with us. Would you bring two chairs and place them by that smaller table by the entryway for them?" Siena added, "The water will be hot for coffee in a few minutes, and Lecheenuss could bring it to the table and join you."

Mochaba went to get the chairs. As he walked into the quiet room, he passed his father's desk and saw Breve's writing quill sitting by the inkwell. When seeing that, he realized he should take a moment and write down his daily notes as his father always did. He reached into his vest pocket, removed a small notebook, sat at the desk, and opened it. After thumbing through the pages, he found some facts and ideas he felt were important to remember. While focused on his writing, Siena's two servants returned and silently walked through the room so not to disturb him. Ten minutes had passed in that quiet room, and Mochaba finally completed his notes. He put the quill down where he had found it and closed his book.

While Mochaba still sat in thought, Siena and Lecheenuss walked out of the kitchen, Siena carrying the tray of fruits and vegetables and Lecheenuss the tray of coffee. As they placed the trays on the table, Mochaba remembered what Siena had asked him to do and placed two chairs by the smaller table. Then he walked to where they had placed the trays on the table. "This looks good, Mother," Mochaba said as he sat down.

Siena replied, "Thank you, Mochaba. Marieka brought these yesterday. The strawberries are my favorite. Supper will be ready soon."

Mochaba smiled to her with gladness as he started sampling the berries.

Meanwhile, Lecheenuss poured their coffee.

Siting by her son, Siena and Mochaba talked about their day. Lecheenuss finished pouring and sat down beside them. Siena mentioned what she had found out at her charity store earlier and wanted to know if Mochaba knew any details about the mysterious couple.

Mochaba raised his cup for a sip and said, "Yes, I know a little bit about that, but Lecheenuss has the details. Lecheenuss knows of some people living near our kingdom who have family in Scotland."

Lecheenuss added, "Yes, the couple I met said they have family there and want to make regular visits here to share supplies with us. We both thought this could be the beginning of something wonderful for both locations."

"Yes, Mother," Mochaba replied, "Munndora trading with Scotland. This could be one positive turning point for ending the resistance between our homeland and theirs. We know Scotland will be difficult, but we think this first step is important. Did you meet with those people today?"

"No, they had left before my visit, but they mentioned to my helpers they would bring supplies every month."

"That's good news, Mother." Then he turned to Lecheenuss and said, "Do you think you will see those people again, Lecheenuss?"

"Yes, I'll speak with them soon."

A few minutes went by as they continued their discussion when Marieka, Raphael, and Rodolfo walked in and joined the others at the table. All talked and laughed about what they had experienced that day and discussed a plan for another orchard to harvest more products.

Still seated, Siena motioned to her servants they were ready to be served, and the two servants brought their supper. One of the servants began spooning food portions on each plate as the other carried in the last two trays of food to the table. Everyone, including the two servants, felt special that evening. The food had been served, and the two servants stood by their table, waiting for anything that might be asked of them. Siena turned her attention to her servants, thanked them for their help, and motioned for them to sit. Then speaking to all, she asked for a joining moment of thankful prayer. They all reached hands to each other and bowed.

"Lord God, thank you for my family being with me and sharing their lives. Guide all of us to follow your grace. Bless this food we are about to share. May it give nourishment and strength to our bodies. Guide my husband and his men to comfort while they follow the path you have set for them and return them home safely. Father, we live by your word. May peace be with us always. Amen."

Marieka looked to her mother and with a smile said, "I love you, Mother."

The others added their loving wishes to Siena before starting supper, and the night went by with the joy of family and friends sharing their lives with each other.

* * *

A few hours after they left Munndora, Breve and his men discovered a freshwater stream along their way and followed it. They all felt relieved when they found it because after a while of riding on horseback, comfortable as it felt, the ride drained their energy. Although they took their time, setting a slow pace, that first day was a warm one and seemed to be fairly long. It was late afternoon when they came to an area by a line of trees where Breve felt it was the perfect spot to make camp. It didn't take them very long to get all the tack off their horses, stake them, and put up their five tents. The soldiers and Eli started looking around the camp for firewood, hopefully pine for starting the fire and birch for long burning.

Herb walked out of his tent to the wagon to get his portable wooden chair and tinderbox with supplies for starting a fire (char cloth, flint, a fire striker, and fibers). After moving a few items around, he found what he was looking for and then walked to the area he had chosen in the middle of their camp. He set up his chair and then kneeled down in front of it to open his tinderbox . . . and discovered the flint and fire striker were missing. *Where are they?* He wondered. Suddenly Herb remembered he had used them a few days earlier to start the fire stove at home and forgot to put them back. He thought to himself, *"Oh well, there're plenty of sticks. I'll make it work."* Shaking his head a brief second, Herb closed the lid of the box and started to look around for wood he needed, pieces that could be used to start a fire by friction.

Breve was at the wagon, removing items and placing them on the ground. Herb walked over and said, "Looks like you're having trouble finding something. Did you forget to bring something?"

Breve reached up to grab the case he had packed earlier that morning. He just looked at Herb and smiled as he set it on the tailboard and removed the straps to open it. After searching through the last of his items, Breve realized indeed he had forgotten something. He felt silly and just looked at Herb with embarrassment. "Yes, I did, Herb. There's no coffee, darn it."

Herb smiled and said, "Ah, I see. Ha! Glad *my* memory works well." Herb reached for a bag on the wagon and said, "Here, my brother, Rodolfo gave me his." He handed it to Breve, but before he released it, he smiled and asked, "By the way, you bring any flint?"

Breve thought for a second, *Hmm, that's an odd question . . .,* and then he realized his brother's kidding was at work. Breve started to laugh as he caught the joke and said, "Ah, you forgot to bring the flint, didn't you? Bet the fire striker's missing too, huh?"

They both started laughing about their silly situation. Breve reached in his case and got the flint they needed for a fire.

The other men had already stacked the wood they had gathered next to where the fire was going to be and then came to the wagon to get their seats and personal belongings before relaxing.

Herb grabbed his brother's chair from the wagon and carried it for him as they talked about things they were going to see in a couple of days. He set Breve's chair down by his and piled kindling and larger pieces of wood with sufficient air gaps to keep a fire blazing. Then setting the char cloth down on a flat piece of wood over a pile of tinder,

Herb stroked his knife's edge on Breve's flint. With each stroke of his knife, the flint sparked onto the char cloth and in no time set the tinder aflame. Ten minutes later, it was a good, hot blazing fire and the signal to start preparing their food.

Breve had Eli get some of their food for them to cook that night and the next morning while he got his coffeepot and filled it with water. Herb went to the wagon and brought apples for everyone. The other men organized all their gear on the wagon till everything had been put away and ready so they would only have to take down their tents shortly after daybreak before they started their early morning ride after breakfast.

While dinner was being prepared and cooking, they all discussed plans for the next day. Soon they had their meal, and then the flames lowered and disappeared as the burnt wood turned to a glowing, hot pit of ashes. After a while, the sky began to darken, the stars appeared, and the three helpers at different times went to their tents while Herb and Breve stayed up a bit longer.

Herb said, "Breve, would you mind if I ask you something about these changes you're about to make? I mean, well, I hope you don't mind."

Breve answered agreeably that he was open to hear the question.

Herb said, "You know I love both you and Siena. You've made a good life together, but, well, it's been quite a while since you've been away from the kingdom. Do you feel okay with it? Is Siena okay with the plans and changes you're making?"

After a bit of silence, Breve answered, "Yes, we have talked about it quite a bit, mostly of how we felt with Marieka and Raphael's plans for going to a new land in the Pacific. It was uncomfortable for us when we first heard Raphael and Marieka speak of it. We didn't know our daughter had that type of interest to explore a land so far away. Maybe it's a good idea; I don't know, Herb. The more Siena and I thought about it and talked it over, the more we remembered how we had started our lives together and how it felt discovering common interests in living our lives together. Yes, Herb, Siena is a brave woman in every way, and I'm so fortunate she is with me about this change. We're glad Marieka and Raphael are willing to give this land nearby an effort. I only hope the place is right for their beginning. Siena feels the way I do with the days ahead of us. We feel pretty good about it. The first year or two for getting supplies won't be easy; I mean Munndora doesn't have all the supplies we'll need for preparing Marieka and Raphael's new orchard. We'll have to get some of those supplies from faraway harbors. There is one port that has most everything. That's Dartmouth; it's quite a distance south. We could do it if we have to, though."

Confident in his brother's answer, Herb said, "I'm glad you understand my question, Breve. And you know what? I feel the same. I want this to work for them too, but promise me something. If other plans need to be discussed and a voyage east is the subject, you let me know. Okay, Breve? That may be the beginning of a whole new dream for all of us."

They both looked to the fire pit, ashes barely glowing.

Herb looked to his brother and said, "Well, looks like my time for sleep. I'll see you in the morning, Breve. Good night." And he got up from his chair and walked to his tent.

Still in his chair, Breve thought for a moment. He looked up into the black sky above to see the constellations glistening. They gleamed brightly through the trees and sparkled as the soft, gentle breeze moved through the branches. A shooting star raced above him through the blackness, speeding fast to the northernmost part of the sky. Breve could see the Big Dipper shine clearly as the star passed through the atmosphere. He closed his eyes and whispered softly as he sat, "Lord and Father Eloah, thank you for my life and this opportunity you have given me. I ask you to direct my life to follow your guidance. Help Siena not to worry and watch over our family while I am away. I follow your guidance, Father. Amen."

Breve opened his eyes and stood slowly from his chair and walked to his tent. He removed some of his clothing, lay in his hammock, and instantly fell into a blissful, deep sleep.

Early daybreak the next morning, one of his men, Marcus, got up and walked to the fire pit. The ashes were cold, but some tinder was still lying there with the flint. He found more dry sticks of kindling nearby and some dry wood. He used his knife with the flint, got a fire started, and then gradually added kindling and more sticks of wood as the fire burned. As the wood turned to hot coals, he took the coffeepot to the stream and filled it with water. Twenty minutes later, he placed the coffeepot on the fire, and when the water got hot enough, he made some coffee.

Several minutes later, Eli woke. Leaving his tent, he immediately walked to the loaded wagon to check everything was secured and ready, except for their tents and chairs that would be placed on the load before they left camp. He found it was secured, then walked to the fire, and stood by it to get himself warmed up a little bit and saw the coffee was just about ready. Markus poured a cup for himself and then another for Eli.

Soon they all woke and came to the fire pit to warm up some and have some coffee.

Herb gathered the flint and what was left of the tinder, put them in his box, and placed it back in his knapsack.

Breve joined the others and shared a small jar of cane sugar cane, passing it to the others to add to their coffee. Then he said to Herb and his men he wanted to start their ride soon after coffee and asked if they had any questions before they left.

They all accepted what they had planned the night before. No questions were asked; just general conversation flowed amongst themselves while having coffee.

Breve's first officer in command partially raised his cup to Breve and said, "I am glad you chose us to go with you on this ride."

Breve replied, "I am too, Lieutenant. Captain Tyrus said you are a good leader of men. I knew he was right when I chose you. You are Lieutenant Gary Vincent, correct?"

"I am honored, sir. Yes, I am Lieutenant Vincent. This man is Corpsman Marcus. Your commands will be done."

Breve raised his cup to him as well and said, "I appreciate your words, Lieutenant. I have the utmost respect for you men." Breve sipped the last of his coffee and said, "Herb and I will take down our tents now and bring them to the wagon. Will you and your men double-check everything for us before we break camp?"

The lieutenant replied, "We are yours to command. It will be done."

The men did so and then prepared the horses for the continued journey. Herb took the coffeepot with him to the stream and filled it, then returned to the fire pit, poured water on the fire, stirred the ashes and embers a bit then repeated all that to be sure the fire and ashes were completely out. Soon all tents were down and secured to the wagon, and all horses were saddled and ready for the ride.

They left their campsite, walking their horses, still following the stream, and taking their time. They were in no hurry because the wagon was fully loaded.

After riding for most of the day, their direction had to change as the stream headed in a different direction. Breve decided they should stop to water their horses and take a break from riding before leaving the stream. He wanted to consider what they might expect through the rest of their ride that day.

They were there about an hour just relaxing by the stream when they noticed a wagon far away in the distance with what looked like four figures riding with it on horseback. Breve and the others stood up to get a better look. They saw it also was coming to the stream.

They all stood and watched.

After several minutes, Breve got a feeling he hadn't had for several years. He could see those approaching were in no hurry, but he couldn't help feeling a decision might have to be made soon that he wasn't ready for. They continued watching—and hearing a constant squeaking noise—as the wagon rolled closer. Somehow that squeaking sound calmed Breve's thoughts a little. Still, he decided to be safe first and walked to his wagon to get his saber and lean it near where he stood. He said to his lieutenant, "This may not get ugly. I don't know, but I'll take no chances here. You men be prepared if this gets bad."

"Yes, we are ready," the lieutenant replied.

Breve said to Herb and the wagon driver, "Sit here and show them we stopped for a break. They may want to do the same; we'll know soon."

Herb and the driver sat down and waited with patience.

Breve and the other two men stood and watched as the wagon rolled closer with its increasingly louder squeaking. He saw the riders were wearing uniforms, but he couldn't tell if they were military or not. The two figures riding in the wagon were a man and a woman. Still though, Breve wasn't taking any chances, and his group looked for any signs of hostility in the men on horseback.

Twenty feet from where Breve stood, the wagon and four riders stopped, and the loud squeak finally ended.

Breve saw it was an older man driving the wagon, and his passenger was an older woman. In a calm manner, Breve walked a few steps closer to them and stopped. It was a quiet moment with tension growing heavy around them all. The man and woman looked a little nervous, not knowing Breve and whom they were facing. The woman suddenly became frightened and glanced downward. The four men on horses looked in silence at Breve. They too, searched for any signs of hostility in movement or words spoken. They showed readiness to fight and protect if needed.

Breve spoke first, "That left wheel sounds bad. Have you checked it lately?"

The old man answered with a calm voice, "It's been making that noise through most of the day. It started shortly after we left camp this morning. One of these men checked it some miles back. We know what's wrong with it but don't have the tools to fix it."

Breve asked, "Have you been on the trail long?"

The man appeared to feel better with answering that question. He said, "Yes, we left our place a few days ago. Since this happened so many miles from our home, we decided that by going slower than we really want, we might be able to make it to our daughter's place."

The woman glanced at Breve as the man completed his answer. Still, though, she remained quiet.

Breve's wagon driver walked up and asked the old man if he'd like him to look at the wheel. The man and woman glanced at each other a moment and showed they wanted some help.

Breve said, "Yes, let my driver take a look at it for you. He's one of the workers at my stables."

The man answered, "Okay," and both he and the woman were surprised as well as appreciative of Breve's kindness.

The driver started examining the wagon's undercarriage and the wheel.

The man asked Breve, "Have you been on the trail a while, sir?"

Breve chose not to mention yet that he was the former king of Munndora. He wanted to clearly understand this man's character first. He answered, "We left Munndora yesterday morning. We're going west to look at some land by my daughter's new property to move close to her."

With a curious look on her face, the woman broke her silence and asked, "You live in Munndora? Our daughter lives near there. We've wanted to—"

The older man kindly motioned to her to not say any more. Breve was a stranger to them, and he felt a little uncomfortable still. He then asked Breve, "Sir, have you lived there very long? Does the owner of that marketplace still have his three boats?"

Breve started feeling more at ease too. He said, "Yes, he does, sir. But he uses all three only when he needs them for the halibut. He likes keeping one docked in case one of the other two stop running. He's learned that using two boats is better than using the three all the time. If one breaks down, his catch drops, and the shelves in their market get bare at times. That's what he says anyway."

The man asked, "There's a charity house near town, isn't there?"

Breve answered, "Yes, Siena started that charity program several years ago."

The man said, "Yes, I heard the king and queen have done well with their kingdom."

Breve walked up to the four men still on their horses. He asked them, "Would you men care to have some coffee with us? One of my men will make a fire." The men looked to each other and then to the older man and woman. The old man motioned to them with a positive, friendly nod.

Herb got up and went to the wagon for his bag and the flint from his tinderbox. Corpsman Marcus went to gather kindling and dry wood for the fire. The lieutenant felt somewhat relaxed but remained alert to all that was happening with the newcomers. Breve handed his lieutenant the coffee grounds and coffeepot and sent him to the stream for some water.

Still feeling cautious, the four men dismounted but remained silent.

Breve said to them, "Men, when I first noticed the wagon and the four of you riding by it, I was uncertain what to expect. I felt positive, but I was still uncertain of it."

Breve's driver completed his inspection of their wagon and said to Breve, "The wheel is close to being unfixable, and that axle needs attention soon, Breve."

A surprised expression suddenly appeared on the man's face. He glanced quickly to the woman and then looked to Breve and asked, "Sir, are you King Breve?"

Breve answered with a question, "Not quite. I was but recently handed control of the kingdom to my son, Mochaba. And your name is . . .?"

The man gave a loving hug to the woman and said, "My name Aeolus, and this is my wife, Athena."

Breve said, "Athena, ah, the daughter of Zeus."

Aeolus replied, "You know Greek mythology?"

"Yes, I've learned some of Greece. Years ago Siena and I took one of our ships to Italy." Breve looked at the reaction on the man's and woman's faces. He could see the tension they felt earlier was gone now, as it was for all of them.

Breve looked to his brother. "Herb, we have new friends. Will the coffee be ready soon?"

The man and woman got out of their wagon and walked over to where Herb sat. He was getting the fire started, adding more kindling and sticks, when they walked up and sat down with him. One of the escorts walked up to the fire carrying good dry pieces of birch wood, placed some on the flames, and sat down with them. Herb thought that was great of him to do that. After some minutes had passed, the fire was ready for boiling water, and Herb set the coffeepot on the fire.

Breve and his men joined the others, and everyone talked. During their conversation, the man told Breve, "Sir, my daughter said when I come to Munndora, I should speak with you about a plan I have."

Breve said, "Have you discussed your plans to anyone yet, Aeolus?"

"No, not till now."

Breve said, "Hold that thought for now, Aeolus. We'll meet and talk about that later."

With some hesitation in his voice Aeolus said, "Okay, I look forward to meet with you later."

Herb put coffee grounds in the boiling water and said, "Coffee will be ready soon."

Breve said, "You say you are looking to move to be near your daughter. Have you sold your home, Aeolus? Or do you want to sell soon? Is it in good condition?"

Aeolus replied, "Athena and I decided to sell our land but have not yet. We're going to Munndora now and brought supplies with us for that charity group there."

Breve said to him, "Aeolus, Siena and I would be happy to help if we could after my return. We're on our way to see property by my daughter's new place. I have some men there now working on it."

Aeolus said, "You are the person who bought that land?"

"Yes, Aeolus, you know about it?"

Herb started pouring coffee in cups for them all.

Breve looked to Athena and said, "I think you'll like this brew. My daughter puts it through a special roast."

Aeolus answered, "Thank you, and yes, I think I know about the land you purchased. Our property is right by a group of builders who are clearing an area for an orchard. I spoke with a few of them a couple of weeks ago, and they mentioned the new owners would move there soon to start planting crops."

Breve asked, "Is that land they're working near the waterfront?"

"Yes, it is. Our land is a fifteen-minute walk from there."

Breve thought for a moment and said, "You mean you have that land just west of theirs?"

Aeolus said, "Yes, Athena and I have lived there many years; it is good land. Our daughter spoke highly of Munndora the last time we were all together. That was quite a few months ago." Aeolus paused for a second and looked to his wife. They smiled to each other, silently confirming they'd made the right decision in relocating.

Breve said to him, "Aeolus, I know the feeling I see in you and Athena. This is a fortunate coincidence. Word about your land is why I left Munndora. I wanted to have a look at it, and here you are, the owners of the land near my daughter's. God is great, isn't he, Aeolus?"

The old couple smiled at Breve when he said that.

"Aeolus, I just had a thought," Breve said, "Excuse me while I speak with my brother, Herb, for a moment." Breve motioned for his brother to walk with him, and after talking for a few minutes, they returned to the fire. Aeolus heard Breve's question to Herb as they both sat down: "Do you feel okay with going back now, Herb?"

Herb agreed.

Breve said to Aeolus, "I've decided to join you and your escorts back to Munndora. I want to discuss your property with you on our way there, and we can help you if the wagon breaks down."

Aeolus said, "That would be kind of you. It will be a slow ride, though."

"That is understood, Aeolus." Then Breve looked to his lieutenant and said, "We'll start back after this coffee."

They talked together for another hour till the coffee Herb had made was gone. It was early afternoon when they put their things away and got themselves ready for the trip back to Munndora. Soon after, they started their ride, squeaky noise and all.

They made it as far as where Breve and his men had slept the night before, set up camp, and pitched their tents. While some gathered firewood, Herb made tinder and started a fire, Athena prepared some food, and two men got fishing tackle and walked to the stream to catch fish. Soon everything Athena had put together was ready. One of the two men that went fishing brought back trout and prepared them for cooking. The whole group had a great meal with easy conversation, and by nightfall, everyone was settled in for a good night's sleep so they could start early the next day.

* * *

THAT FOLLOWING DAY the kingdom of Munndora was busy as usual. The market opened a half-hour late because a new catch of salmon and cod had just come in. Daniel's two boats were loaded with the fish.

Siena slept in a little that morning. After waking and dressing, she went to her kitchen to make coffee but saw there was coffee already made for her, so she poured herself a cup. She walked to her table and saw a note from Marieka, asking her to come to her garden when she could later that day. Although welcoming the idea of visiting Marieka, Siena felt it would be better to go the following day because she had tasks, including work at the charity building, to do first.

After she finished her coffee, she went to the charity building and took inventory. A couple of hours later, Siena walked back to the castle and met with her maids and servants to present a new schedule.

By early afternoon, all her tasks had been completed, and Siena decided it was time to prepare dinner. Then, feeling tired, she just wanted to relax. The night hours soon approached, and Siena slept well.

The third morning waking up without her husband by her side, Siena felt rested, but she missed hearing his voice. It was about seven thirty when she opened her eyes and just lay there for a little while. Then she got dressed, planning to visit Marieka after breakfast. She got some berries, bread, and a few vegetables and made coffee. Soon she finished her meal and started planning her day. She felt she should go to the market later. Feeling more awake now, she strolled to the garden and saw Marieka, busy talking with a couple of people, but interrupted her conversation to greet her mother. Siena smiled in return. Noticing berries on a table, she decided to sit and have some while her daughter was occupied.

Marieka soon finished with her customers, then walked over to Siena, and gave her a loving hug. "I'm glad you came by this morning, Mother. Have you seen Kylia yet? She came here yesterday and mentioned she had some new yarn for you."

Siena replied, "Yes, I thought I'd meet with her on my way home later. How are you today, sweetheart?"

Marieka said with happiness, "I'm doing well, Mother. When do you think you'll be back home?"

"I should be there by four, I think. Is there something there you need, Marieka?"

"No, I was just curious."

While they talked, another customer came to Marieka's garden.

Marieka said Jana had mentioned that she looked forward to seeing Siena again and visiting a little while.

Siena got up and said, "I have to go to the charity building again today. I'll be there a while. When I'm done, I'll stop by again to see you and then go see Kylia. She'll be at her market this afternoon. Please say hi to Raphael for me."

"I'll do that, Mother. And I'll save these berries for you to take home later. I'll come by and visit with you tomorrow too."

"Okay, sweetheart." Siena gave Marieka a hug then left to the charity building. She soon finished her work and walked to the marketplace.

On the way, she saw Kylia and caught her attention, and they walked together in friendly conversation.

"Here's the yarn you requested, Siena," Kylia said.

"Thank you."

"How was supper that night?" Kylia asked.

"It was wonderful having family there. That was a delicious salmon recipe you gave me. The next time I have them over, I'd like you and Daniel to be there too."

"I knew you would like it," Kylia replied. "And we would be happy to come over."

When they arrived at the market, Siena said, "Good talking with you. I'll visit you soon."

"I look forward to it," Kylia said.

Siena walked home and Kylia went in the market to finish her day.

The first footman greeted Siena as she walked up to the castle's main door. She thanked him and went to her chambers to put on something more comfortable to wear for the rest of the day. One of her chambermaids came in and said there were fresh sheets on her bed and asked if she would like the throne room fireplace to be started for her. Siena set the yarn down and berries and said that sounded good. The maid left to find one of the porters to start the fire.

Dressed more casually now, Siena took the yarn and berries to the throne room, already warming to a relaxing temperature. After putting the yarn away, she went to the kitchen for a cup of cool water and then sat in the throne room. As she ate the berries, Siena thought about her husband and how she missed him. She felt lonely and prayed he would be back sooner than he had planned.

"I need to start a new craft project," Siena said to herself, got her knitting needles and yarn, and sat in her rocking chair near the fireplace. She didn't start anything right away but just closed her eyes and thought of what she wanted to create. *Something Breve would like to have to help keep him warm on a cool evening. I'll make a pair of warm socks.* She opened her eyes and started knitting while rocking and humming quietly.

A servant came into the room and, seeing the flames starting to diminish, placed more wood on the fire and then left the room.

By the time night was falling, Siena had finished the toe in the first sock and was working her way to the heel. She held it up and examined it closely. *Yes, it'll be perfect for Breve,* she thought. She got up from her chair for a break and walked to her kitchen to have a refreshing cup of drinking water and then returned to her knitting. When a servant entered the room to check the fire, Siena asked if she would make sure the fire remained hot during the night for her. The servant agreed as she put more wood on the fire and then left the room. Siena continued to knit, feeling proud of her new creation, even though it was just a pair of socks. She knew, though, Breve would be grateful for them as a reminder that she would do anything for him. This she knew would make him happy.

All of a sudden, as if all Siena's thoughts and prayers of love and of family were answered, in walked Breve and Herb with smiles on their faces. But she worried, *Oh my, what happened?*

Breve said, "Hi, honey." Then turning to Herb, Breve said, "Herb, go ahead and use that spare room I mentioned to you earlier. I'll have our cooks make something special for us tomorrow. Good night."

Both Breve and Herb looked so tired. Herb walked by Siena with a smile and a friendly wave hello to her as he passed.

"I'm sorry for the surprise, hon, but I hope it's a good one," Breve said. "I told Herb he could stay here tonight. I hope that's okay. We're both pretty tired."

Siena jumped up out of her rocker with excitement and gave her husband the most passionate hug she had ever given him. Tears of true love and happiness had developed when she realized this was no dream. Siena said, "Oh yes, Breve, my love. You know I understand. I missed you so. Is everything okay? Are you all right?"

"Yes, it is. We rode for a day and a half, and whom did we see on our path? The man and his wife who own that property next to the plot we gave Marieka and Raphael. The owners were on their way to Munndora to visit one of their daughters for a few days and to see if Munndora was right for them to move here. What a great couple they are. We all rode together to Munndora and just now got back. They're meeting with us tomorrow to finalize our purchase of the new property, hon. I made him a fair offer, and they are happy with it. It's our new home now, Siena. I mean it will be after we meet with them tomorrow."

"Oh, I'm so happy you're home, my husband. Would you like to have some of that fruit juice I have left for you?"

Breve walked closer to Siena, and while he hugged her gently, he said, "No, that's okay, hon. I'm glad to be home with you. I want to give our thanks." They closed their eyes as Breve, with humility in his voice and wisdom in his words, said, "Father Eloah, you are the truth. I place my faith in Jesus Christ. I believe him to be the Son of God who died for our sins and rose from the dead to give eternal life. Guide our lives, Lord, to live for you, the author of eternal salvation unto all mankind. Thank you for giving me the Holy Spirit to follow your guidance and wisdom for the direction in our lives. He is my friend, and he is my helper. Thank you for my family, Lord. Please guide my sons and my daughters through the many challenges they will find. In Jesus's name. Amen."

They opened their eyes together, and with a whisper to her husband, Siena said softly, "I love you, Breve. Thank you."

"It's been a long day, and I feel a little tired."

"I'm tired too, my husband. A warm sleep does sound good." As they walked together talking, Siena said, "Breve, I want to try one of Kylia's recipes tomorrow for our supper. Let's invite our family."

Breve agreed.

They climbed into bed and soon fell into a good night's rest.

The next morning, Breve and Siena woke to a beautifully colored sunrise peeking over the hills and trees around the kingdom. They could tell it was going to be a nice sunny day. Wishing each other a good morning, they got out of bed and prepared for the day's few meetings before they met with the landowners.

Siena wanted to go to Marieka's garden and see Jana and her daughter and to visit with her friend Kylia at the charity building. She decided to walk that day again rather than go by her carriage. Breve wanted to meet with Captain Tyrus and set a date to start loading one of his ships with supplies for his and his daughter's new properties. With that settled in the afternoon, Breve left the docks for his castle. There, he walked to the throne room in preparation for the purchase of his new land from the landowner, Aeolus.

Breve made some coffee and sat at his desk to study some documents. Soon after, one of his servants walked in with Aeolus. Breve got up to get another cup and offered him some coffee. Aeolus mentioned again to Breve that he and his wife were selling their property so they could move to Munndora to be near their daughter. Breve explained his decision for the new land and added that he would have Mochaba help Aeolus and his wife build their new home. Soon the papers were signed, and Breve and Aeolus finalized their meeting. Before Aeolus left the castle, Breve said that Siena would be happy to meet his wife and asked him to come back the following week before his ship left for their new property.

Siena came back home a little later that afternoon and found Breve looking tired. He was sitting in his throne relaxing. She thought as she walked with quiet steps, *I hope the meeting went well.* He opened his eyes and said he had met with the landowner and now the land was theirs. They could go to their new place any time after next week. That made her so happy. He added that Captain Tyrus would have their ship ready to load next week or any time afterward when they wanted.

Hearing that also made her so happy. With a sweet gentle voice, Siena said, "Oh, honey, you look exhausted. Here, my love, here's your favorite seat cushion. Do you feel all right? Would you like some coffee before we have supper, honey?"

"Yes, that would be nice, but I don't need it right away," Breve answered.

With a cheerful sound in her voice, Siena said, "I want to change into something cooler to wear, and when I come back, I'll make something for us. Here, I'll get some coffee for you. I'll be right back, hon."

Still seated, Breve smiled brightly and thought to himself, *I am so lucky to have Siena in my life. Thank you again, Lord.*

* * *

MARIEKA ALSO SOON RETURNED to her home. When she opened their front door, she was so surprised seeing Raphael already there, and she smelled a delightful fragrance when she entered their main living room. He didn't cook very often, but this evening, he was preparing one of her favorite meals. She said, "Mmm. Oh, honey, how did you know that I was so hungry for this delicious meal? I brought us some berries that my mother picked today too." She set her basket on the counter and gave Raphael a tender kiss.

He added the last ingredient and said, "It's just about ready, hon. I bet you both had fun today. I hope she is well. While you get ready, I'll set your plate."

Giving him a bright smile, Marieka walked to their bedroom to freshen up and put on some clean clothing. She was so thrilled that Raphael had made their supper that evening. It wasn't very long before she walked back to their table and sat down. She said, "Thank you so much, sweetheart. You're wonderful for doing this. I was feeling kind of tired, but this really helps me feel good, honey."

Raphael showed her a big smile as he walked to the table bringing her some fresh drinking water. "It's my pleasure, sweetheart."

He walked back to their kitchen and returned with a warm bowl of the main course. As he set it on the table, Raphael said, "I know you have been so busy with everything that we have all been trying to accomplish, Marieka. You deserve to relish this time and to relax, sweetheart." Then he leaned over and gave her a loving kiss. "I love you, Marieka."

* * *

AT THE CASTLE, after Siena gave Breve his coffee, she began preparing supper. Breve soon joined her in the kitchen, wanting more coffee. Siena reached for his cup and said, "Here, Breve, I'll get that for you." Breve gave the world a relaxing yawn and said, "Did you and Marieka have a good day?"

Handing him the coffee cup, she answered. "Yes, we had such a wonderful day today. I met the helper that works with her too. She's such a nice person. Her name is Jana. She studies medicine, and Marieka helps her with her studies. Our daughter is so smart. Don't you think so, honey?

His bright smile showed he agreed. Then Breve said, "Honey, I was thinking about our lives in our early years again today. Most of those days were sure exciting for us, weren't they, hon? You were happy with the choices we made, weren't you? I mean, we always talked about things before we chose what we did. You were happy we did it that way, weren't you?"

"Oh, yes, so very happy," Sienna answered.

Breve continued, "The landowner I met with earlier, Aeolus, built their home and lived there for seventeen years. It is good property. He said he and his wife will be moving near their daughter's home here in Munndora. The offer I made him was a fair offer, and our new land is ready for us."

Siena stopped preparing for a second, set down her spoon, and walked slowly up to Breve. With a passionate look in her eyes, she hugged him tightly and said, "You are my love, the love of my life. I thought the same as you about this whole thing. Tonight, I wanted to ask you something. I wanted to prepare your favorite supper myself tonight for us to share and to see how you felt about it. Marieka asked me earlier today for us to live with them temporarily while we all build on that land. I'm so happy you went to buy that land and so glad it didn't take the two weeks we thought it would take. Being Marieka and Raphael's neighbors makes me so happy, honey." She reached for the coffeepot and poured him more coffee, saying, "Here, my sweet. I'll have supper ready soon for us. Would you set our table, please?"

He gave her a loving kiss and said, "Be glad to sweetheart. I'll be in there."

Breve got some dishes and silverware to set their table, and when finished, he thought to himself just as he sat down, *This is like our new beginning again, Lord. Hold us tightly in the grip of your grace for I feel your guidance in this for our lives. Yes, journey onward.*

He realized he had forgotten drinking cups so returned to the kitchen. After getting the cups, he passed Siena and said, "That smells delicious. The table's ready. Let me know if you need help, okay?"

"It's almost ready. Go sit down, and I'll be there shortly."

Several minutes went by, and Siena walked in carrying a tray of appetizers and freshly baked dinner rolls Breve liked so much. She placed the tray on the table and walked up to her husband, giving him a loving kiss, and said quietly, "I love you, honey." Then she went back to the kitchen and returned with the savory aroma of planked salmon with chopped almonds and lemon. She placed it on the center of the table and sat near him.

Breve smiled, reached for her hand, and said, "My darling, I'm so happy you are in my life. I love you, sweetheart."

Over supper, they talked about their day and all the details that needed to be addressed for the upcoming changes in their and their family's lives.

After finishing their supper, Breve cleared the table for Siena and cleaned the kitchen. Siena walked to their chambers, picked up her favorite adventure book, and started reading. Half an hour later, Breve walked in and got ready for bed too. Siena reminded Breve that Marieka and Raphael should be there the next day about midday to see them, and she thought that Mochaba and Lecheenuss would be there soon after. Breve replied that he looked forward to seeing them. They said good night to each other and soon peacefully fell into a deep sleep.

* * *

THE NEXT MORNING, Marieka made some fresh coffee for her and Raphael. They sat at their table and talked for a little while. She said she felt very confident that her mother and father would join them in their new land. Marieka gathered both their cups and walked to the kitchen sink to clean them before they left their home to spend that morning organizing the new supplies that had been brought to her garden and to offer help at the market if it was needed before meeting with Breve.

Jana was also at the garden, and the three quickly completed all the work. Marieka asked Jana if she would watch over things there for the day while she and Raphael went to the market for a while. She said she would be back to close later. Jana replied that she would be happy to take care of the garden for her.

When Marieka and Raphael arrived at the market, they saw Lecheenuss and her father, Daniel, with his crew unloading his fishing boat of the day's catch of seafood. For two hours, Marieka and Raphael helped them, and when they had finished, Daniel wrapped a twelve-pound salmon and gave it to Raphael for their help. Resting for a minute, the couple walked over to Lecheenuss and asked if she and Mochaba were going to the castle later too. Lecheenuss said yes; they both planned to be there that afternoon. Marieka said she would talk with Lecheenuss there later.

While they still had time before needing to be at the castle, Marieka and Raphael walked back home to freshen themselves and relax. A short time passed, and they left to see her father. During their short walk to the castle, they talked about their dream for harvesting products they grow and using Munndora as their main port for export to other lands because of its location.

As they approached the main entrance of the castle, Marieka and Raphael opened the door to a pleasing fragrance. They walked in and saw her mother just then passing through that big main entry room on her way to the main living quarters. She looked as if she was in a hurry, but when she saw the couple, she suddenly stopped. With a big smile, she walked up to them and gave them a loving hug. She said, "Your father is in the throne room anxious to see you both. Go on in now. Lunch will be ready very soon. I'll be right there."

She left them, and the couple walked through the hallway that passed the castle's main kitchen while enjoying that delightful aroma. Without missing a step in their walk, they both slowed their pace and closed their eyes for a few moments. When they reached the kitchen's open doors, they paused as if in a trance. With a deep breath, they inhaled slowly to capture the savory aroma of freshly baked bread. They both opened their eyes and peeked into the kitchen as the cook was removing the fresh breads from his brick oven.

"Mmm, ahhh, warm, fresh bread," Raphael said. "Maybe pancakes too?"

Marieka gave him a soft elbow jab, and they both smiled with thoughts of enjoyment. In a few minutes, they entered the throne room where they saw Breve setting the last of the silverware next to a fine china place setting for six on Siena's new linen tablecloth. Breve smiled and said enthusiastically, "Good morning, my family. Please have a seat. Mochaba and Lecheenuss will be here soon. I'll get the coffee." Then he walked back to the kitchen.

With puzzled looks on their faces, Raphael and Marieka sat down at the table. Just then, Mochaba and Lecheenuss walked in with their mother. As Mochaba and Lecheenuss sat down at the table, Siena walked out of the room to help Breve bring their coffee. The four sitting at the table talked about their new lives and enjoyment of just being a family together. Several minutes passed, and then Breve and Siena walked back to the table, each carrying a silver tray. Siena carried six coffee cups and a small bowl of fruit. Breve was carrying his prized silver and gold coffeepot that he had won racing horses' years before. With it was a bowl of Mochaba's favorite powdered cocoa that Marieka made. They set the trays down on the table, and Breve began pouring their coffee while his wife handed each cup to them.

With broad smiles, Breve and Siena sat down in their chairs and raised their cups together. The four others also raised their cups.

Then Breve said with joy, "This is to our family for, no matter where we are, we will all be as one. Here's to you, my sons and my daughters."

They all drew a sip from their cups.

Breve stood up from his seat and said, "Here's to you King Mochaba, Queen Lecheenuss."

With silent gladness, they all stood up from their chairs as tall as they could, raised their cups high, and with proud respect, they gave a soft cheer and sipped from their cups before they all sat back in their chairs.

Suddenly, as if on cue, three servants walked in with trays and served their meal.

Casual talk began while they were eating, and after several minutes, Breve became more serious. "Mochaba, my son, your mother and I felt it was time to give respect to the new king. It should start now, this afternoon. So we wanted to have this meeting with a good meal and to talk. Raphael, Marieka, yesterday Siena and I bought some land located along the channel not far from your property. It has a home on it, and we both will be moving there as soon as we can make it possible. We'll be your neighbors, Raphael, and help you build." He smiled to his wife and then to Raphael and Marieka. Then Breve added, "Oh, we almost forgot to mention something. You have a new home on your property now too. The men I hired some time ago completed your new home three days ago, and it's ready for you to move in when you both are ready." With a slight cheer, Lecheenuss and Mochaba along with Siena and Breve raised their cups again, and they all felt the warmth and joy of each other's love.

Well into the afternoon, they all talked more about details and ideas for the first harvest. Satisfied with their plans, the three men helped their wives carry the dishes to the kitchen and cleaned things up. Breve mentioned that he would be ready when they came to the castle and meet him tomorrow before they would go to the docks and see Captain

Tyrus. After they all finished, the three women gave their husbands a gentile hug and said thank you for their help.

Before long, Raphael and Marieka left the castle to go to her garden and spend the rest of the daylight hours arranging products and selling to the people. Mochaba and Lecheenuss stayed only a little while longer and finally left saying to his parents, "Thank you, Father. I will help our kingdom always. We are so pleased you will be with Marieka and Raphael when they start their new harvest." They all hugged and said their goodbyes, and then Mochaba and Lecheenuss left and went to their home.

The next morning the sunrise was so beautiful. It seemed like a perfect day to begin the plans for their move. After having some coffee, Raphael and Marieka left their home. Marieka went directly to her garden and got her stand ready for the people. In between attending to customers, she continued making a thorough supply list for the trip.

Raphael went to see Breve so they could walk together to the docks and see the captain. On the way to the castle, Raphael happened to meet Mochaba just before they got to the main entry. They walked in together and saw that Breve was also ready, so all three headed to the docks, talking and planning their days ahead.

While they walked, Breve said to Mochaba, "Captain Tyrus is looking forward to seeing you, Mochaba. He's the best officer of this land. When he and I talked things over yesterday, he said he would help you understand better about shipping supplies, whether imported or exporting, from this harbor. You will need his help for a while, son."

As they all walked up to Captain Tyrus, Breve said, "Good morning, Captain. These are my sons, Mochaba and Raphael. Mochaba is your king now. Siena and I will be joining Marieka and Raphael on our move to the property I mentioned to you a couple of days ago."

The captain saluted his new king and said with all due respect, "Your orders will be fulfilled, King Mochaba." He began explaining his duties at the docks of organizing the ships coming to port and said, "I will help you, My King. Any questions you have, please ask me, and I'll help you."

Mochaba answered, "I will have a lot of questions during the days ahead, Captain. My father speaks very highly of you. I look forward to learning everything about the duties of shipping imports and exporting supplies here in Munndora."

Breve walked with Raphael alone to discuss the plans of their voyage and said, "We want to help you and our daughter, Raphael. That ship you see here is the one we will be taking. I have a meeting with one of my advisers soon. Rodolfo will be here soon to do the inspection of this ship for me before we take it. He said he could use some help with that, and I want you to help him with it."

Before Breve left the docks, he told Mochaba about the meeting he was going to have with some representatives about a new shipment and that he would be back at the castle to finish with his record books and meet with several of his other merchants about shipments scheduled to arrive in Munndora after he moved. Breve suggested Mochaba watch Captain Tyrus for part of the day to see how he maintained his harbor and help him when he could. Finished with his instructions, Breve said, "We'll talk later, okay? Have a good day, son."

Mochaba followed his father's suggestion, and after several hours watching the captain work with his men on the docks, Rodolfo showed up to begin the inspection of their vessel. Mochaba told Raphael he needed to take care of some important matters in town and wouldn't be back to meet with him. Knowing his cousin's way in doing his work thoroughly, Mochaba added that it might take a couple of days for Rodolfo to complete his inspection. He mentioned that Rodolfo was there now and Raphael should watch what he did and help him when he could in getting the ship ready for the journey.

From a short distance away, Rodolfo waved to Raphael as he walked up to Captain Tyrus to see if there were any details he should know about before he started his inspection. Raphael couldn't hear the words being spoken with the captain, but a couple of minutes later, Rodolfo nodded his head and then departed, walking towards Raphael. As Rodolfo approached, he reached out to shake hands with Raphael and said, "Hi, Raphael. How's Marieka? I was hoping that Lieutenant Vincent would be here now to help me, but the captain just told me he sent the lieutenant to get some supplies. I could use some help with this inspection. Will you help some, Raphael?"

"Yes, Rodolfo, I'll be glad to help you."

"Great. Come on, Raphael. I have to get my logbook for this vessel."

They walked and talked together about important points of inspections that ensured the safety of a vessel before leaving the docks. They arrived at the deckhouse ship supply building and geared up with a length of rope and a few tools, along with the logbook for Rodolfo's final report of survey. Rodolfo gave Raphael the few tools and kept the logbook and rope, and then they walked back to the docks to begin their work.

At the ship, Rodolfo said to Raphael, "Glad you're here to help me, Raphael. You'll learn some things that are vital to these heavy vessels. I think you're going to like this one. She is one of the finest ships on the sea. This inspection will take a couple of days. It's actually a lot of fun. Don't hesitate to ask questions while we go through this. I'll be happy to explain as we go if you like. I spoke with the captain, and he mentioned that Lieutenant Vincent needs my help later. For now, let's get the tools and rope we need and get started. We'll do the outer hull structure from bow to stern today. We'll finish with the main deck and sails tomorrow."

Rodolfo set the rope down and had Raphael supply him with the tools he needed and to help make some measurements for calculating the weight and mass of the large vessel. His inspection also included the condition of the ship's new rudder. This was Rodolfo's main concern. After several hours, their job was completed. Rodolfo wrote his approval for all sides of the ship's outer hull enclosure and rudder.

Rodolfo gathered the tools they used and the sections of rope in a container by the ship. He said to Raphael, "Your help makes this job easy. Truly it helps. I'll be back in the morning fairly early, and we'll finish the rest, starting with the main deck. Tomorrow will be a long day. Thanks again, Raphael." And Rodolfo started walking to find the lieutenant.

It was still daylight as Raphael left the docks and walked to town, slowly making his way back home. While walking, he decided he would cook something that night for Marieka, and he stopped at different places to pick up a few things for their supper. Soon after, he was back home and started preparing their supper. Marieka walked in just a few minutes later, and they talked about their day. After supper, they relaxed the rest of that evening and then retired to bed.

The next morning, Raphael got up early and prepared to go back to the ship to help complete the inspection. After making some coffee, he got his packsack, put a few snacks in it, carried it to the table, and sat down while sipping some coffee and thinking about something.

Marieka walked in a little later to have some coffee too and said, "Good morning, sweetheart." While she poured herself a cup, she saw some cocoa near where she was standing. She carried it to the table and sat down. With a happy glance as she spooned some cocoa in her cup, she said, "Are you going back to meet with Rodolfo now?"

"Yes, we'll be finished today. He has a lot of experience inspecting these ships. I've learned a lot about the importance in correctly following and completing the many steps and logging the results in the records. I like being part of it."

Marieka got up suddenly from the table saying, "Oops, I forgot something for you." She walked to their kitchen and opened a cabinet where she had a container of fruit juice that she had made the day before. She got some wrapping material and wrapped the container to help keep it cool for a few hours. Returning to the table with it, she set it in Raphael's packsack to carry with him. Marieka said, "I think you're going to like this juice I made yesterday, hon; it's delicious."

"Thank you, Marieka."

They soon finished their coffee. After rinsing their two cups, Raphael walked with Marieka to her garden, giving her a quick kiss, and said, "I'll be at the docks for most of the day. See you home later. Have a good day, hon." Then he walked to the docks.

There he saw that Rodolfo had just arrived and was getting the tools they had left in a container by the ship. Raphael said, "Good morning, Rodolfo," as he reached for the other tools and rope they needed, and then both walked up the gangplank talking to each other about continuing their inspection. They started their inspection right away with the areas aboard the main deck—a very thorough inspection starting from the large holding tank containers for potable, fresh-water supply to the galley. The quality of all sections was Rodolfo's focus for insuring safety and comfort for all aboard when at sea. All areas—from the officers' privy area to the cargo holds and storage rooms, the medical room, and all quarters used by personnel—had to pass the inspection. They spent the full morning completing that part of their inspection.

Next, they moved to the rigging and connections to the most important part of the vessel. They would make certain the connections to the three masts and all sails that would be used on the open seas were safe and undamaged. Rodolfo said, "Inspections of the rigging are vital. We'll start there, Raphael." They began with the foremast before going to the main mast and then to the mizzen. As the inspection continued, Rodolfo explained to Raphael in great detail the importance for this part of his inspection and that it would take a while. He repeated that he was very glad Raphael was there to help him. They continued their inspection with all line stays of the foremast and jib boom, fore topgallant stay, outer topgallant stay, inner topgallant stay, outer foretopmast stay, inner foretopmast stay, forestay, martingale stay, and finally the bobstay. Next they went to the main mast and continued their inspection, repeating all steps they had just completed on the foremast. Several hours into their work, they decided it was time to take a break, so they walked to a shady area on board and sat down to have some lunch and talk awhile.

Rodolfo opened a container near them and reached in to grab some food he had prepared earlier that day. He offered some to Raphael and said, "Here you go, Raphael. Sorry I forgot the beverage. Will you and Marieka be going to your new place soon?"

Raphael reached for his sack and pulled out the juice Marieka had given him. He said, "Ah, and it's still fairly chilled as she said. Here you go, Rodolfo. I'll share it with you. Yes, we'll be leaving when Breve and Siena are ready to go. They acquired some property a couple of days ago, near where we're going to be living. We'll be neighbors." Raphael took another sip and continued. "There's a lot to this inspection. I'm glad to help. I've learned quite a bit today. I see how important it is to be thorough, or it may cause safety problems later. This means a lot to me, Rodolfo. Thanks for showing me all the details of a proper inspection."

Rodolfo replied, "Thank you, Raphael. You're a good student. We'll be finished in a few hours.

They spent the next fifteen to twenty minutes just talking together of all the new plans that were being made for the kingdom and the new properties.

When their break was about over, Rodolfo asked, "You ready, Raphael?"

Raphael nodded his head in agreement.

Rodolfo replied, "We'll be finished soon. Let's get back to it."

Continuing from where they had left off, they worked on the final mast, the mizzen. As with the others, they checked its strength and condition, all the stays, and then the condition of all its sails—the mizzen royal sail, mizzen topsail, and last, the spanker sail, located on the aftmost mast. They left that mast and walked back to the foremast and checked the condition of its sails—the foremast royal sail, the foremast topgallant sail, the foremast topsail, and finally the outer and inner jibs. Then they did the same with the sails of the mainmast. Finally for the last part of the inspection, they thoroughly checked all compartments. They started from under the bow deck to the captain's cabin. It took two hours, and conditions were all good for passing inspection. Rodolfo said he needed to finish the last of their inspection. It would take only a few minutes to check the wooden blocks, tackle, and the tie downs for the ship's rigging. He had missed three and should check them. Also he added that the usual allowance for turning measurements from the funnel to the place of setting up in the channels was on his mind and important. Those needed to be done to complete their inspection before they left the ship.

After the second day's inspection, Rodolfo wrote his approval of acceptable satisfactory condition and safety for the entire vessel's outer shell and all inner compartments, all three masts, and all sails and rigging. He asked Raphael to meet him the following day to help organize the supplies that would start coming aboard for a test shipment to a location nearby. He said it would take just a couple of days, and then the ship would return to Munndora.

As they walked the gangplank and off the main deck, Raphael said, "Watching the professional, thorough way you do the inspection of this ship was very inspiring, Rodolfo. This has been an honor. Helping you makes me feel as important as the ship. I learned over these two days the importance of a thorough inspection for any vessel shipping out on the open seas. Being assured of the safety and comfort of a vessel is very important. I understand some of this now. What you meant in having fun with doing this job is very encouraging to me. I'm glad I could help you with this inspection, Rodolfo."

"Thank you, Raphael," Rodolfo said. "I'm glad to do this for all of you. I've been a part of ships a long time. I love sailing. For now, I have a few things to take care of with the lieutenant, and later I'll be meeting my father. I'll see you here tomorrow."

It was still daylight as Raphael remained by the gangplank. Then as he turned his attention to the main deck, he decided to go on board again. He was fascinated by what he had learned and the way Rodolfo had completed his inspection of this vessel.

Raphael stood for a short moment and then began walking the deck to become more familiar with this new experience. While he walked, he noticed the captain approaching the gangplank on the dock below and standing there for a minute as if looking for someone. Then the captain began to walk up the ramp to get onboard. Raphael thought he might be looking for him, so he walked to the ramp.

The captain stepped on deck, faced Raphael, and said, "Sir, I felt that right now while I have a moment before my next ship arrives would be a good time to meet with you and make certain that you understand I'm here to help you. When you need something done, it will be done. Just let me know, and I'll take care of it for you. I'm helping my king and family and getting this vessel ready for your departure. After speaking with Rodolfo a minute ago and studying the report of his inspection by you both, I am confident your departure will be soon. By the way, Raphael, Rodolfo said he will be going with all of you. He said that he will talk with Breve about that."

With a modest reply in his voice, Raphael said, "This is all fairly new for me, Captain. I confess that having Rodolfo with us would ease our minds when we leave this port. Will you be part of the crew too when we ship out?"

Tyrus replied, "No, sir. King Mochaba will need me here for now. My second in command will be joining you, though. He's a good officer. Breve knows him well. Rodolfo just left to help him with the final gear you'll need onboard. They both should be back here soon, I think; might be tomorrow, though. Your father-in-law found a good crew that knows this vessel well. This is a good ship! I know she'll get you to your new home safely."

Seeing in the distance the next ship he was expecting, the captain said respectfully, "Sir, I see my next ship arriving now. I must get some things ready for her before she ports. Sir, you have a great rest of your day and please say hello to your wife for me."

Raphael reached to shake hands with him and replied, "It's an honor to meet you, Captain Tyrus. I'll tell Marieka you said hi."

Returning his respects to Raphael, the captain thanked him and said that Raphael would meet his lieutenant soon. He added that Rodolfo had told him that he and the lieutenant might have to ride to town and build the few parts needed for their ship's new rudder. "Rodolfo is a specialist," he said, "and he knows these vessels well. He helps with the repairs. I'm sure they're finishing that part now. I just spoke with Breve, and this ship will be ready very soon. Sir, my supply ship will be docking soon, so I had better go now. If there's anything at all you need done before shipping out, please let me know. Have a good day, sir." The captain turned and walked down the gangplank.

Raphael said, "Captain, I look forward talking with you again. May the day be right for you and your family too."

When the captain got to the dock, he turned and said, "Thank you, Raphael," and then went to make ready for the incoming supply ship.

While standing by the ramp, Raphael looked around and saw Mochaba walking towards the ship. He thought, *This is that special blessing Marieka and I have dreamed of. It's really here now.* He closed his eyes. *Thank you, Lord. Thank you.* Then he walked down the gangplank, leaving his ship. Raphael felt confident that the man he had just met and spoken with would help him understand shipping and sailing.

When he reached the dock level, he joined Mochaba. As they walked, Raphael said, "My King, I'm glad to see you. I'd like to discuss with you our plans for the crops Marieka and I will be harvesting as soon as we can. Can we meet and talk later today? I have a good plan, but it will take some time before our first shipment arrives here."

King Mochaba thanked Raphael and felt encouragement in this new way of living for him and his queen. He said, "I look forward to seeing your plans develop, Raphael. I know my sister well. She is so happy being with you. I'm happy seeing that too. Queen Lecheenuss and I are anxious to see your dreams starting to build with more land and more crops. We'll miss you both as we will miss Mother and Father. I'm ready to see the women now, Raphael. How about you? Come on, let's go see them."

They walked around the dock a moment to see if Breve was near, but he was not, so they left. As they walked, they discussed more ideas regarding Munndora as the main port for shipping supplies and this new move they were organizing. Raphael admitted to Mochaba that he felt a little nervous, that he had so many different feelings about getting things ready.

Mochaba said, "Raphael, my friend, I'm glad you said that. I wasn't sure how to admit those same feelings. There are many questions I have too, now that I have my kingdom. I talk with Lecheenuss when I want to share my thoughts. She helps me think things out. Talk with Marieka. I know she's eager to help anytime."

They approached the main doors of the castle when suddenly both doors opened. Siena and the two younger women were just leaving. Everyone was surprised to see each other at that moment.

As they were leaving, Marieka said to Raphael, "Hi, honey. I'm on my way to the garden. I have to get some coffee and talk with Jana. Mochaba, I'll be taking Raphael with me. Mother and Lecheenuss are going to the market. See you later."

King Mochaba went with Lecheenuss and his mother while Marieka and Raphael went to the garden. Marieka asked if her father had spoken to him about when they would be able to go to their new home. Raphael said he hadn't spoken with him since earlier that day but he knew it would be soon and that Rodolfo and the lieutenant were finishing all the repairs to their vessel. Raphael said he was very encouraged meeting the captain and impressed by his organization in preparing their vessel's voyage.

When Marieka and Raphael got to the garden, Jana was at her table, focused on writing in her tablet. With a big smile, Jana looked to Maricka as she laid down her quill pen beside her writing pad and said, "There, I finally found the solution to that formula I talked with you about a few days ago, Marieka—the one about the curing power of jellyfish. You need to process it in a certain way to remove all the poisons from it first before it is flash-dried in that final stage. It was so simple. I don't see how I missed not finding it for so long." Looking at Raphael, she said, "Hello, Raphael. I have coffee made. I'll get us some."

Marieka and Raphael got a couple of chairs and sat at her table. Jana returned with a tray of three cups of the fresh coffee and some fresh milk she liked with hers.

Marieka said to Jana as she sat down, "I know how it feels, Jana. Isn't it funny how discovery is found when we're determined to find the answers? Persistence and patience, we all have both and more, right, Jana?"

With a big gleaming smile, Jana said, "Yes, thank you, Marieka."

Raphael smiled too and politely said, "Jana, soon Marieka and I will be leaving Munndora to our property west of here and start cultivating the new land for our crops. We'd like to know your feelings about being here, being in charge of this garden, and helping to organize the harvest when the crops are shipped and delivered."

Marieka joined in and said, "Yes, Jana, we all are wishing that you will be comfortable with that. But knowing that you also help with the kingdom's medical needs, we don't want you to feel that the harvest is more important than anything else. I can find someone to be here if your focus will be only on medicine. I hope you understand that what you choose will always be respected. I do hope, though, that you wish to be in charge of our products and supplies when they arrive here."

Raphael agreed with Marieka's decision and said, "Yes, Jana, you won't regret being in charge of the kingdom's new supplies."

Jana was so pleased to hear what they were asking her. She said, "Yes, I want to be a part of your business and watch over the shipments when they arrive. I'm happy you both feel good about me doing this and helping organize the harvest for us."

Marieka said, "I'm happy you're with us, Jana. I've always admired your accountability and character, and you've taught me so much about nutrition and medicine. I feel the same as my husband. You won't regret being a part of our business."

Jana took another sip of her coffee and smiled.

They continued talking while they finished their coffee, and soon Marieka said she wanted to get home early, so they all cleaned their area, closed the garden, and left for home before it got dark.

As Jana walked home, she started thinking of the opportunity she had now. The more she thought about it, the better she felt. When she got home, she opened the front door and saw her dog, little Pugsee, watching her father prepare supper for his family. Pugsee was happily wagging her tail. Tyrus stopped stirring food in the pot for a minute and picked up a little morsel of food from the counter. He said, "Watch this, Jana. Little Pugsee is so smart."

Pugsee started moving her head from side to side and rocking her body back and forth while wagging her tail in excited anticipation of the morsel.

Tyrus got the dog's attention by making clicking sounds with his lips. Holding the morsel up, he said, "Pugsee, Pugsee, UP! Up, Pugsee. UP. Yes. Now sit, Pugsee. Sit! No, not roll over. No. . . . sit, Pugsee. Sit. No, no. Pugsee, not roll ov—ahhhh. . . . no! Sit, Pugsee, sit . . . oh well. Here, Pugsee. Catch! Yes, attagirl."

Still smiling, Tyrus looked toward Jana and said, "I think I spoke about her accomplishments too soon. She's such a sweetheart little girl, Jana."

He directed his attention back to Pugsee, "Go lie down, Pugsee. Go on, go lie down now. Yes, good girl, Pugsee. Your mother and I have so much fun with her, Jana."

Tyrus walked back to the pot and continued stirring and cooking their meal.

Jana moved closer to her father and smelled the beef stew. "Mmm," she said, "that smells so good, Father."

"I'm glad you like it. Your mother will be home soon. She asked me to make something delicious for us tonight, and it's almost ready." Then Tyrus asked, "Did you see Raphael and Marieka? He said he wanted to ask you something."

"Yes, they came to close the garden early today, and we talked together for about an hour. They asked me if I wanted to be part of their produce business and be in charge of their shipments when things get started. I'm happy they feel good about me doing that."

Still stirring, Tyrus said, "You are good friends, and knowing Marieka and her family, I'm sure they were counting on you being with them. You're their best choice. Will you be going to their new property?"

Just when Jana was about to answer his question, her mother, Leana, walked in after a long day in the apple fields. On her way to change into clean clothing, she said, "Thank you for cooking tonight, honey. Mmm, that smells so good. Did you make your secret stew? Hi, Jana. I saw Marieka earlier today. She said for me to say hi for her if she didn't see you today. I'll be right back."

Tyrus answered just before Leana entered their bedroom, "Yes, I did, hon. I'll be ready soon. We'll set the table for you." Then he placed the pot of stew on a trivet on their table while Jana added some coffee, plates, bowls, and silverware.

While they waited for Leana, Jana said, "No, Father, I'll be here in Munndora continuing with my responsibilities with our people and the garden too."

Tyrus said, "Sounds like you could be pretty busy. Be sure to ask me to help you when work becomes too much. Okay, sweetheart? The port was certainly a busy place today. Breve, King Mochaba, and Raphael were there too. They're getting everything ready for their move. I'm helping them with that too."

Finished cleaning up, Leana came to their dining area and joined them. She and Jana sat down at the table, and Jana started pouring each of them a cup of coffee and said to her mother, "I did see Marieka and Raphael earlier. We just closed the garden before I got home. They're so kind and friendly. Marieka's a wonderful person to work with."

Tyrus came to the table carrying a tray of fresh bread. After he placed it down by the trivet, he started ladling his stew into their bowls, then sat with them, and they started having their supper. During the following minutes, it was so quiet until Leana said, "This supper is delicious, honey."

Jana said she was happy to have such wonderful parents.

Leana and Tyrus looked to each other deeply, and Tyrus said, "We're so happy you're the person you are, honey. You've learned so much in your studies of medicine. Everyone in Munndora is so thankful of that."

Talking about the things that were discussed earlier that day with Marieka and Raphael, Jana mentioned she was pleased the shipments were going to be her responsibility, and she felt her parents would help her learn correct ways to organize the business of import and export.

Tyrus and Leana said they would always help her, and Leana added, "I could be the person doing the records for their harvest and keep track of things for you. It would be a relief doing that, rather than working with only apple orchards. Can I do that for you, Jana?"

"Yes, Mother. I'd love to have you help me." After taking her last bite, Jana looked to her parents and saw the two most loving people she knew. She appreciated they had raised her to accept people for who they are and to follow her instinctive nature when experiencing new things in her life because not all uncertainties in life are bad.

After supper, Jana and her mother went to the main room. Tyrus followed them carrying a tray of fresh coffee. After he set the tray down on a small table, he left to clear the dining table and clean up in the kitchen.

Meanwhile, the two women began planning the business of harvesting and shipping crops. Jana opened her writing tablet and started listing the ideas by priority, including several suggestions from her mother. When Tyrus finished cleaning the kitchen, he poured himself a cup of coffee and walked back into the main room to offer his ideas about important aspects of Jana's and his wife's new jobs. The three spent the rest of the evening making plans.

* * *

THE NEXT MORNING, Captain Tyrus went to the docks. As usual, he went directly to the dock house to pick up the papers he needed and started scheduling his duties for the day. He got to the pages his lieutenant had written and realized that he and Rodolfo had worked most of the night before in finishing repairs to the ship's rudder. The notes indicated it would be ready by the end of the day. Tyrus gathered his notes and walked out to oversee the repairs to the rudder. Approaching the ship, he saw Rodolfo just getting out of the water to where the lieutenant was standing on the dock. Gary handed him a towel as the captain walked up to them.

"Good morning, Captain," Gary said. "Did you see my notes? We were lucky in finding the parts we needed. Rodolfo does know this vessel well. I'm glad we have him, sir."

For the next several minutes, the two talked about the repairs and the full day's distance the vessel would be traveling.

Finally dried, Rodolfo joined them and said the rudder worked perfectly now and the parts were in place. He also mentioned the importance of these new parts, why they were needed, and said, "Captain, I would like to take the ship on that short delivery you scheduled for the *Rover*, a two-day test cruise of the repairs. I may have to make some adjustments before Breve takes her. Just want to be certain she's ready.

The captain agreed and then asked when the vessel would be ready for loading some last-minute supplies for the voyage. Rodolfo said a day after the test trip and ready for boarding personnel one day after that.

Captain Tyrus replied, "That's good news. Good job, Rodolfo. Lieutenant, meet with me, say, in four hours."

Later that day, Breve came to the dock to check on things. He and the captain talked as they walked to the dock house. The captain said his lieutenant and Rodolfo would be finished with the repairs later that day and they'd take it out for a two-day test cruise the following day to make sure the ship was ready.

The service his captain supervised brought a smile to Breve's face. "Thank you, Captain, for all your service for this kingdom and our family. You have been a tremendous help supervising and keeping order on this dock. I'm glad you are here. You're a good friend too. This shows me you will help my son with sound skills and advice in shipping while he learns being the kingdom's leader. I know he'll listen to you, Captain." He then shook hands with Tyrus and said, "My wife thanks you, and I thank you, Captain."

They both had coffee and talked more about the voyage. In the middle of their discussion, Lieutenant Vincent walked in.

The captain said, "Hi, Lieutenant. Come in; pull up a chair. I'm glad you got here when you did. We're planning some things that involve you."

Gary found his cup and poured one for himself, added some cocoa, and then brought a chair to their table and sat down.

The three men discussed the repairs that had been completed.

Tyrus asked Gary, "Are those worn sails replaced? Is she ready?"

With great confidence, he answered, "She's a new ship again, Captain. Her final repairs were all completed, and she's ready for her test. In the next two days, we'll see how she maneuvers while we deliver that shipment. We'll test that rudder repair thoroughly, sir. Rodolfo is one darn good specialist in this work, I'll tell you. I am glad we have him, sir."

Captain Tyrus asked his lieutenant to spend the next couple of hours preparing the docks for the busy day they were expecting to have the next day. When that was completed, Tyrus suggested Gary take the rest of the day off and catch up on his sleep. Gary soon finished his coffee and left the dock house. Breve and the captain stayed and went over the logbooks in detail to finalize the plans for everything that was needed and to be loaded on the ship before she left Munndora. Two hours passed, and they left the docks with confidence that all was organized and would be ready.

While going back to the castle, Breve saw Mochaba and Lecheenuss finishing their task with Raphael and Marieka and walked up to them, saying that he wanted to talk with Mochaba about their leaving Munndora soon. He asked all of them to walk to the castle with him and talk over dinner. When they arrived, the cooks had everything ready to serve their supper. While they were having their meal, they continued discussing their plans. Breve mentioned to Mochaba that when he wanted more knowledge about shipments coming to or leaving Munndora, Captain Tyrus would be more than happy to help him.

The men and their wives soon finished supper, and all stayed at the table relaxing and talking. Marieka and her mother walked to the kitchen and brought more coffee to the table. As Marieka poured for everyone, Raphael said this was an exciting time in his life. He looked forward to going to their new place. This had been a dream of his and Marieka's throughout most of both their lives to have more acres for orchards and field crops. He mentioned also that he heard Rodolfo might go with them when they leave Munndora.

King Mochaba then stood up from his chair. Raising his cup high, he gave Raphael and Marieka a toast of thanks and his wish that their dream would be fulfilled with their new property. He said that Rodolfo was welcome to go with them, but only if Herb gave his permission. The others raised their cups and cheered with him.

Such a memorable evening, Siena thought to herself, seeing her family all together like this. She then said she had rooms prepared for the four of them and invited everyone to sleep over for the last time together before leaving Munndora. All agreed and gradually left for their assigned rooms, sleeping comfortably throughout the night.

The next morning after breakfast, they went their own ways. The four travelers made final preparations for their items to be loaded onto the ship after she returned from her test run. Raphael and Marieka walked past the docks on their way to her garden and saw that the ship

Rodolfo and he had inspected had already left on the test voyage delivering some supplies near Munndora.

Over the next two days, everyone checked and rechecked their personal supplies and made sure they had listed everything they wanted to take and had prepared some livestock they would take with them also.

Two days passed, and the ship returned to port. Rodolfo filed his approval of the vessel and reported to captain Tyrus the ship was sound and perfect with no problem found during the test run. On that day, the crew, captain, and lieutenant began loading all supplies for the travelers. Breve and Mochaba supervised to make curtain everything was ready to go aboard and was properly stored away. The next and final day, everyone met at the docks. It was a beautiful warm, sunny morning, and the travelers were all ready to go.

Mochaba walked up to Breve and asked to walk with him and talk privately for a minute. Mochaba said, "Father, we will miss you and Mother here. I realize this first year will be a challenge. I hope it will not be a difficult one for you, though. When can Munndora expect your return for more supplies and a visit with us?"

Looking into his son's eyes and seeing Mochaba's love of his family, Breve replied, "You are my son. Your mother and I are so fortunate you are in our lives. We will miss you too, you and lovely Queen Lecheenuss. You have grown to become a good and honest man and a fine leader of inspiration, my son. I can only say for now I will miss you and we will come again. This first year will be a busy one for all of us. Several months may pass before our ship returns for more supplies here, possibly a year; I don't know that answer yet. Supplies in Munndora are not as abundant as at other harbors, so when a change of plans is required, arrangements will be made. This I know: we will return."

Mochaba was silent for a moment and then said, "Father, you will always be the king in our hearts and in our lives. We look forward to your return when it can be done."

Breve gave his son a hug of respect and said, "You are truly a great spirit of a man, my son. Your mother and I are very proud of you. You will be missed." Breve showed him a smile, and they both walked back where the other travelers stood, talking together.

The ship's crew was just completing their final inventory and inspection of the vessel's cross-braces, the ribs added by Rodolfo and the crew. When the captain gave his clearance to proceed, the crew then continued inspecting the vessel's rigging, food supplies, and grain and oats for the few livestock that were onboard. When Captain Tyrus was sure everything was being completed, he walked off the mighty ship to meet with Breve and the others waiting. He said with confidence that the ship would be ready for them to board very soon, adding that he knew the vessel will get them to their destination safely.

Breve thanked him for making sure everything was inspected and secured and ensuring their safety before they left Munndora. The others joined Breve in thanking the captain and talked together to make sure they were all ready to leave their kingdom.

Everyone was anxious and ready to get on board and start the voyage. Finally, one of the crew walked down the gangplank and said to Breve, "She's ready to board now, sir."

Breve and Raphael saw Herb and Rodolfo walking to the ship and waited for them. All four—first Breve, then Raphael, Herb, and Rodolfo—walked up the gangplank. When they reached the main deck, Breve turned to Herb and gave him his thanks for letting Rodolfo go with them. Breve then turned his attention to Raphael and said to him, "Raphael, give the order to board, and let's start our voyage."

Raphael turned around to face the others on the dock below, and with inspiration in his voice, he called to everyone, "All aboard!"

The travelers on the dock started up the gangplank one after the other as well. In no time, they were all aboard. Herb and Rodolfo helped the crew remove all the tie offs from the cleats on the dock to make ready to leave. When they finished doing that, Herb turned to his son and hugged him, saying, "I will miss you, my son." Then to the whole group, he said, "All be safe."

Herb walked down the gangplank and turned to watch with the others as the vessel readied to leave the port. While the crew removed the mooring lines from the ship bitts on deck, several of them manned the oars, and the large vessel slowly began floating out to the bay. When it cleared a short distance from the docks, King Mochaba yelled out with both hands to help carry his voice, "Bon voyage, my family!" He and Queen Lecheenuss waved to them on their safe and happy two-day voyage.

Once the ship reached the middle of the bay, the crew stopped rowing and then quickly but carefully climbed the ship's three masts to let down its sails and begin the voyage. Mochaba and his queen continued standing on the dock with Captain Tyrus and watched as the ship's sails quickly filled with the soft breeze, and then slowly but surely, their vessel began to sail away through the channel straits, leaving the kingdom of Munndora for her travelers to follow their dreams on their voyage west to their new property.

Those on shore watched the ship float into the distance till it could no longer be seen. King Mochaba and Queen Lecheenuss then left the docks, walking with Herb and sharing their thoughts. When they got to the castle, Herb said goodbye to them and continued to his place.

Mochaba asked Lecheenuss before they walked into the castle, "Honey, what do you say we make some fresh coffee in the kitchen of our new home?"

They walked through the large main entry doors and noticed the fresh and familiar pleasing fragrance that filled the air. They'd been through these hallways and rooms many times before, but never was the freshness as pleasing as then.

As they continued walking through the castle, King Mochaba said, "I love it here. I'm glad you're here with me, Lecheenuss, my queen."

Lecheenuss smiled; her king showed her so much love. As they continued walking together, Lecheenuss looked around with pure joy and happiness in her heart. When they came upon one of her favorite wall paintings of her husband's family, she said, "Oh, I love this painting, Mochaba." She pointed to a figure in the painting and said, "I've stopped and looked at this painting several times. I get a different feeling with this person. I see a kindness in his eyes that my grandfather had. He was a very strong man yet so sincere in caring for others; he had such a loving way in living. Such a generous man to others, he was my father's father. I remember him well. Oh, I miss him so. Mochaba, I stop here, and I see in this picture the strength of the man's spirit of reason. Was this man your grandfather, the king who founded Munndora?"

With a smile, King Mochaba turned to her and said, "Yes, he was my grandfather. That is King Sodamunn. Father said he was a man of great courage and honor. He lived with integrity, always took the righteous path, and found trustworthiness in others. The people recognized him as a man of peace in giving respect and justice to all. Father said Grandfather had joined the navy and left after twenty-four years on a quest with others to find new shores. It took them almost one year to find the perfect place. When they found this land, they knew it would be their new home and started building. I feel I knew him through the words Father said about his father—about the skills my grandfather learned, the encouragement others gave him, and the responsibilities they taught him for leading people. He learned to be a great leader, and he was a great leader."

Lecheenuss looked more intently at the depiction of Sodamunn, lost in thought.

After a moment, Mochaba said, "Come on, hon, let's go make some coffee."

Before reaching the kitchen, they stopped at the throne room. When they walked in, they saw on the table a covering of amazing colors that Siena had left for them. Surprised, Lecheenuss stood for a moment looking at it.

King Mochaba walked directly to the throne and sat in it for the first time in his life. Relaxed sitting there, he thought how comfortable it felt. The surroundings in the room helped him to relax even more. He soon started to get a little sleepy, closed his eyes, and for a few minutes, just let his mind drift to things his father and mother had taught him through the years. While deep in his thoughts, he whispered, "Thank you for the trust you have in me, Father. I will make good with all my decision." Opening his eyes, he saw his beautiful queen walking to her new rosewood table and chairs. Mochaba said, "Honey, that *is* such a beautiful table!"

Lecheenuss gave Mochaba a loving smile and then turned her vision back to the table. It was covered with the most beautiful damask cloth she had ever seen before. On it was a silver tray setting, and on that tray, there was a folded paper in the middle with two empty cups and a plate of cocoa powder sitting beside it with a yellow rose lying beside them. Lecheenuss sat in the chair closest to the folded paper and reached for it thinking, *I wonder what this is.* Suddenly she retracted her hands. *Wait. There're* two *cups here. That could only mean . . .* Mochaba needs to be here so we can read it together. She went to Mochaba and said, "Honey, would you sit at the table with me? I think your mother left something for both of us to read. I think we should see it together. I'll go prepare that coffee and something refreshing for us before we read it." She walked to the kitchen and began preparing a snack for them.

Still a little sleepy and in his thoughts, Mochaba stood up from his throne and slowly walked over to the table. The closer he got to it, the more he noticed and admired the craftsmanship and caring skill in making it. Not wanting to dirty the fine damask tablecloth, he walked to a nearby cabinet and got one of the place mats to set on the table for Lecheenuss.

A short while later, she walked back carrying a tray of assorted vegetables and fruits with two cups of fresh coffee. She placed it on the table and sat next to him.

With a hug, Mochaba kissed her softly and said, "Thank you, hon."

They both sat there for several minutes sipping their coffee, giggling as they talked and being silly together.

Then Lecheenuss reached for the note again. She brought it close to her heart and looked to Mochaba. She said, "Okay, honey. Are you ready?"

He nodded his head yes.

She unfolded the paper and began reading it aloud.

Our dearest Lecheenuss

We are so very happy you are part of our family. Mochaba is such a happy man knowing you are with him. Breve knew Mochaba was now ready to lead the kingdom our family has governed for generations. We both are so grateful that your parents are our lifelong friends. While we're away, we will be thinking of you and Mochaba always. You are a blessing to us all.

May inspirations follow you always. Please send our love to your parents. Tell Mochaba we know he is ready.		We love you.

Siena

Breve

Finished reading, Lecheenuss sat with silent thoughts for a moment, and then her eyes began to tear happily. She said, "I love you, my king. Siena and Breve have such beautiful spirits. I feel so blessed knowing them. You are my life, my husband, my king. I will please you always."

Mochaba softly brushed a tear away from Lecheenuss's cheek and said, "You are the love of my life, my queen. I am so blessed having you with me. I will cherish you forever. I love you, Lecheenuss."

They both stood up and hugged each other passionately without saying a word. Then they looked into each other's eyes, and in an instant, they knew their love for each other would last forever.

That afternoon they talked about how to help their kingdom. They would begin the following day with planning improvements for better roads and storing up lumber and rock.

* * *

MUNNDORA WAS A PRODUCTIVE COMMUNITY with many people. With her father's encouragement about their market and the shipments coming into port, Queen Lecheenuss learned better communication skills that helped make the improvements in their land and the charity services Siena had been involved in. Before long, seven ships loaded with products were coming into port twice a week on a regular basis.

Captain Tyrus soon promoted two qualified men to help him keep up with his busy schedule. Queen Lecheenuss was such an intelligent woman in organizing the commodities for their land. Within one year with help from her husband and father, she eliminated hunger in the entire region.

Mochaba learned and accomplished much for his kingdom. With manual labor from his people, the improvements of their land continued as months passed. During that first year of King Mochaba's reign, he developed better, longer-lasting, and more accessible pathways in and around his kingdom. The new roads resulted in safer and more reliable transport of supplies and easier everyday travel for his people.

Periodically, the people would select a representative to meet with the king and negotiate plans for payment to the people working with him for the progress of their kingdom. Before each job was started, the king and his representatives would have their meetings for determining the cost for the project, and at times, bartering would be used for the people in the negotiations. King Mochaba's main goals were to protect and improve his people's wealth and safety and to build a strong community. One afternoon, Mochaba met with his two advisers and said they needed a greater quantity of cobblestones and other rock for the new pathways. Inspections around Munndora and outlying areas were made periodically for lumber, earth, and stone products. When needed products were found, the workers immediately started gathering and storing them. Before long, there was a large quantity of stones, stored and ready for future use. When lumber was needed for building solid structures, the king would organize a number of people to cut some timber. He would always go with them because he loved working outside. Rain or shine, he would be there and cut timber with them. Not many trees were cut down at one time, though, only what was needed for that project. The number of trees cut was always recorded because for every one tree that was cut down, two young trees were planted to replace them. That would help keep the trees plentiful and their forest green.

The development of the land continued like this throughout that first year and into the second year.

* * *

One evening while King Mochaba was relaxing at home having supper with Lecheenuss and enjoying his cup of coffee, he mentioned that Raphael's first shipment should be coming to port soon. They both were so happy thinking about that. Lecheenuss asked Mochaba if he thought his parents would be onboard too. He replied that they might be on it, but knowing his father's adventuring ways for discovery and his age, he felt his father might have stayed to fulfill his passion of exploring on dry land.

Lecheenuss said, "Oh, I hope their plans were fulfilled. I was so excited for them the day they left."

After taking another sip from his cup, Mochaba said, "I remember Captain Tyrus saying to me that Breve's group had already started planting crops. I mentioned it to you some time ago, but I didn't know the details at that time. I just hope the reality of the new place met their dreams. I'm sure we would have heard otherwise by now if it didn't."

"I am sure it did—and still is doing so," Lecheenuss replied. Then she got up from her chair, walked over to Mochaba, and with a loving hug, said, "I'll make us some more coffee."

King Mochaba felt so wonderful when she did that. Then he reminded her of what his sister had said before they left—she and Raphael would start developing orchards and begin planting crops as soon as they could. Then the finest quality of crops and coffee would be shipped as soon as possible. She mentioned it might begin in the first year. That was her target, but the first shipment could take two and a half years. Their plan was to have Munndora be their main port for delivery with one shipment every year. From there, both King Mochaba and Jana would inventory and export a percentage of each cargo to ship to other locations.

He and Lecheenuss talked more that evening about it and felt certain the ship would arrive sometime soon. They both smiled with loving memories of family the more they talked about it. At a late hour that evening, they both decided it was time to go to their chambers and have a good sleep.

* * *

IN THE MIDDLE OF THE NIGHT, the king suddenly woke. He realized right away that his queen wasn't there with him. A short time passed, and he began to feel that something was wrong. With a chill in the room, he thought, *This isn't like Lecheenuss.* With a loud voice he called out, "Lecheenuss, Lecheenuss. Are you okay? Where are you, my queen? Say something!"

There was no answer. Several minutes had passed. He repeated his words again. Still no answer. He got out of bed, and while he dressed, he repeated his words again but louder. Still, there was no answer. He began searching for her. He looked in all the rooms near their chambers; all were empty. The king became more worried. He slowly walked to his throne room. She wasn't there either. Mochaba then sat down in his throne to think quietly. He began to feel the emptiness inside and worried even more. While deep in his thoughts, he started to get very tired. He tried staying awake, but several minutes passed, and slowly he closed his eyes and fell into a deep sleep.

At daylight, the king woke and opened his eyes. He stood up from his throne with positive thoughts of his queen and walked to their chambers thinking that everything was okay and she would be in bed sleeping peacefully. He got to the chambers, and she wasn't there. Now he felt so worried. Mochaba got his cape before leaving the room and started to walk out, but with a glance, he looked over to her dresser and saw her crown resting beside her mirror. He walked over to it and carefully picked the crown up. He held it in both hands and slowly turned it as if to examine every line. Seeing every detail of its features, he began to feel a strength from inside. While he gazed at her crown, he decided to keep it with him, thinking it would give him strength and help him find her. He put it under his vest near his heart and walked out of their room thinking to himself, *Everything's going to be all right.*

It took some time to search every room in the castle. Almost an hour had passed. Lecheenuss was not there. Mochaba felt so bad. He stopped and calmed his emotions for a moment. He quietly said to himself, *I need to clear my thoughts and plan something. I have some coffee and a cup in my saddle bag. I'll get a coffeepot before I leave here.*

Now outside, he walked to his stables and saddled up Argento. Still deep in his thoughts of what had happened during the night, he put the coffeepot in the saddlebag, then got on his horse, and slowly rode through town looking for a sign of where Lecheenuss might be. Still he saw nothing. *Oh, where can she be? Where have I not looked?* He chose to ride to the place where they were both happiest, the place by the stream where they were married. Finally there, he dismounted and made a fire by the stream. After filling his coffeepot with some water, he set it on the fire and sat down beside it, thinking, *I pray you are all right, my love. Where can you be?*

When the water began to boil, he added the coffee. After several minutes, he poured himself a cup and calmly began thinking about what his father would do to find Lecheenuss. As he sipped his coffee, his thoughts gradually became clearer.

Suddenly Mochaba remembered something one of his people had told him a long time ago about a woman he had met and talked with for only a few minutes. She was a pretty woman, and at first, the man had thought he knew her. But when he had walked up closer to her, he had realized he'd never seen her before. He had thought, *Hmm, I'd like to know this person, I think.* So they had talked. The man said they had been talking for only a few minutes when suddenly he had felt a nervousness he had never known before. He admitted that talking with a new woman to whom he felt attracted might do that. But in this case, all of a sudden, without words being said, he had noticed a cold stare in her eyes. He saw bitterness there that he had not seen before. The man described it as a feeling of something that could cause misfortune to all around her. His knees had become a little shaky, but physically he had felt fine otherwise. There had been no pain at all; he had just felt very tired and somewhat confused in his thinking. He said that his thinking had become clouded, his vision had become unfocused, and his eyes had started to feel so very heavy for sleep. All this had started at once, all at the same time during only the few minutes she and he had been talking. The man said the feeling he had experienced was so strong that he just had to walk away from her as quickly as he could. When he had done that, everything he had experienced minutes before had disappeared; it was as if it had never happened. Everything had returned to normal.

Mochaba never saw the man again. He took another sip from his cup as he thought, *Wait a minute. Could this be something like that? My queen has no enemies. She has always helped others. Is there someone that would do this to me? Hmm.* Still in his thoughts, Mochaba took another sip.

After a while, he set his cup down on a stone and then stood up on the meadow of green in the spot where they had been married. Mochaba reached under his vest for Lecheenuss's crown and raised it high to look at it. With thoughts of his love for her, he turned it slowly and focused his sight on every line on it, praying to himself that she was well and feeling inside himself that it would help find her. He knelt down and reached for his cup while now holding her crown tightly against his chest. When he stood up again, he looked towards his kingdom and the areas around it with sadness in his heart. Then suddenly he yelled, clearly and with determination, louder and louder with every word, "Lecheenuss, my love, you are my life. Lord Eloah, our Father in heaven, please protect her. I will find you, my love. I will never stop looking."

Still standing, lost in his feelings, Mochaba again held up her crown to look at every detail. Softly he said out loud, "I did not foresee this, my love. You have vanished. I have searched our kingdom a great distance and am unable to find you. I have never before felt the fear I now have. I need you, my queen. You are my strength, my queen, my love, my wife. I pray you are safe and unharmed. Oh, Great Father, where is my queen? Please see she is safe and lead me to her." Mochaba lowered his head and prayed silently, *Lord, please, help me find her.*

Overcome with sorrow, the king put out the fire and carefully put the crown back under his vest before riding back to his kingdom to search the grounds again. He felt more at ease now that he had taken some time to calm his thoughts and think things out.

He needed help in finding Lecheenuss. Mochaba couldn't shake off the fear that she might be hurt somewhere and not able to get back home safely. He hoped it wouldn't be much longer for the ship he was expecting back to finally arrive, and then the crew would join the rest of the people to help him find his beloved queen.

Despite getting the help of the townspeople and his servants in his search, Mochaba could not find her. The whole kingdom was saddened.

* * *

THE YOUNG WOMAN the frightened man spoke of was Jayabella, and she knew the king well. She had hidden Lecheenuss where she could never be found and had cast a magic spell upon her.

Jayabella's powerful spell had caused Lecheenuss to leave the bedchamber in the middle of the night. She had remained in a deep sleep and felt no pain or fear; she had just gotten out of bed and walked out of the castle. After a long while, her steps had slowed and become very shaky, but she had continued walking, as if she was in a dream. The early morning daylight appeared, and still she had kept walking. Reaching the forest near the kingdom, Lecheenuss had gone into it as if a great magnet was pulling her.

Through the trees, she had walked and then come to a large meadow with many different colors of plants all around her. There she had finally stopped, slowly knelt down by a fallen tree on the carpet of green, and fallen into a very deep sleep.

* * *

TWO DAYS AFTER THE DISAPPEARANCE of Lecheenuss, the ship finally arrived at Munndora with its first shipment of supplies. The ship had first stopped at Ardmore Point to deliver some supplies and to finalize an agreement Breve made with the port authority there. This had made their arrival take a few extra days before docking at Munndora. The crew had not learned what had happened to the queen.

After docking their vessel, the crew immediately began unloading their cargo. An hour passed, and King Mochaba arrived to welcome them. A short time later, the crew finished loading their wagons and were then ready to deliver their supplies.

Lieutenant Vincent and Rodolfo walked down the gangplank and off the ship to greet King Mochaba. They were so happy to be back. The lieutenant gave his salute to Mochaba, and then he walked to Captain Tyrus, who was nearby, to give his report. Rodolfo mentioned to the king that the coffee they brought was a better harvest than what Munndora was used to, not a lot better, but still the harvest was a good one.

As he spoke, Rodolfo noticed that Mochaba was troubled. He asked, "Are you feeling okay, Mochaba? Is there something we can do to help you?"

Controlling his emotions but with watering eyes, King Mochaba looked to his cousin and said, "Lecheenuss has vanished. Two nights ago, I woke up in the middle of the night, and she wasn't there with me. I didn't think anything was wrong at first, but after I called to her several times and she didn't answer, I got up and started looking for her. A while later after searching all the rooms and not finding her, I started feeling a fear that I've never known. I've looked everywhere for her in all places that I know, Rodolfo, and I can't find her. She's my strength. She's my life, and I'm worried she might be hurt. Will you help me find her?"

Extremely concerned, Rodolfo answered, "You are of my blood. Yes, I will help you, My King. After we get to your castle, we'll unload your supplies and meet with you in your throne room. I'll explain about this shipment we brought you. And then we'll take care of finding your beloved queen; she'll be home soon, Mochaba."

The king immediately felt the heavy weight lift from his mind and said, "Thank you, Rodolfo. You have no idea how happy I am to have you here with us. It is as if your vessel was supposed to arrive at this time. We've all missed you. How's my family doing? Is everyone okay?"

Feeling the joy of returning to Munndora, Rodolfo also smiled. "Yes, My King. We've all missed you too. The voyage took a few days, and we were all happy to finally make it there. The fertile grounds are good. There were traces of other people who had lived in some of the nearby areas, and we spent quite a bit of time at first planning and then clearing land for the orchards and other crops. The land is good where your sister and Raphael planted their crops, and Marieka is making the best of it. I do know that she and Raphael still think about that land in the Pacific waters.

King Mochaba thought a second and then asked, "What do you mean, Rodolfo? Is their property not what was expected?"

"Oh yes, they are happy, and Breve and Siena have a nice place too. They all said to say hello to you and Lecheenuss for them. There is good land there; it just needs time to get things in peak production."

When they arrived at the castle's storage house, Rodolfo and the king dismounted. The crew started unloading their wagons, and the king began walking his two horses the short distance to his stables. He gave the horses to the stable hands, who removed the riding gear.

Mochaba thought, *I'm glad Rodolfo is here to help me.* He decided he would soon know after their meeting what Rodolfo meant and walked to the castle with full confidence a good plan would develop soon. Knowing it would be a little while before Rodolfo would be available, Mochaba walked to his chambers and removed his cape. While there, he remembered his wife's crown. With loving gentleness, he set it back on Lecheenuss's dresser and then went to his throne room.

A few minutes later, Rodolfo and two men of his crew entered the room with a few bags of their cargo. Mochaba was curious. While he sat in his throne, Rodolfo explained that Marieka and Raphael were correct about their property. "Your parents both invite you to come to see them someday. Mochaba, you—both you and Lecheenuss—really should go see them when you can." He said the crops and other supplies they brought back were better because of Marieka's skills for growing more nourishing plants. Then he described her recent discovery. Marieka used the oyster shell and a few different plants that can only be found in the sea in a precise combination that has proved to be the answer she had been seeking for a long time. Rodolfo said the discovery Marieka found was partly Jana's idea, and it helped in the preparation process for the crops. "Very soon, My King, I will show you what I'm talking about. These supplies are better."

Then their discussion turned to Lecheenuss's disappearance. Talking with Rodolfo about what had happened wasn't easy for the king. Mochaba explained some details and mentioned uncertainties he'd let build up and control his thoughts for a while. He told Rodolfo of the special place where they had been married and how he had ridden to that place hoping that would help him think more clearly. That is where he found peace in his thoughts. Mochaba said, "The coffee I made there helped me think clearly with every sip. That was so encouraging when I noticed how my concentration improved tremendously as I sipped the fresh brew from Marieka's coffee. Knowing you and your shipment would soon be here also helped me to be calm in my thinking. It never happened like that before. The coffee did help me."

Hearing Mochaba talk about not finding Lecheenuss told Rodolfo he had gotten to Munndora at the right time. He began giving Mochaba all the details of this new shipment. Rodolfo mentioned the ongoing inspections done to insure the high quality of the produce. Then he said, "Mochaba, I feel positive that Lecheenuss is safe. What we have brought to you in this first shipment, My King, is Marieka and Raphael's best harvest so far. There is only one way, though, for Queen Lecheenuss to be set free from wherever she is right now."

Rodolfo reached into one of the sacks that he had brought with him to their meeting. He said, "My King, here is the answer. Take these fresh roasted coffee beans that your sister prepared for you and go to your kitchen and make a pot of coffee. Make it a strong brew." Rodolfo put some of the coffee beans into a small empty pouch he had with him and gave it to Mochaba.

Mochaba said, "Rodolfo, you say this brew is better than before. How will this roasted coffee help me find my queen?"

He replied, "You'll see something good here, cousin Mochaba. Soon the sweet aroma of this new roasted brew will fill the air in your kingdom. I'll be right back to help you make the coffee, but I have to see my crew for a minute." As he and his two crewmen were getting ready to leave the room, Rodolfo said with a sudden smile, "King Mochaba, Queen Lecheenuss will soon be with you."

Mochaba walked briskly to the kitchen and immediately placed the special coffee beans in the coffee grinder he had made. In no time, he was brewing the first pot of his sister's new discovery, trusting in his sister's knowledge and Rodolfo's word. The coffee began to release its pleasant aroma. It soon filled the air in the kitchen and then traveled throughout the castle.

Rodolfo returned to the kitchen with another pouch of the coffee beans, and as he set it down on the counter, he said, "My King, your sister has mastered a better roast for the coffee bean. That discovery was the beginning of a special process using her spices and herbs that she holds secret. This is her medicine for the coffee. The coffee bean is nourished daily with her new secret. As the coffee bean is going through the roasting process, her secret ingredients are added and help intensify the beans' natural aroma. Some beans actually increase in size while going through that process. Marieka calls those her treasures for coffee. The fragrance will travel great distances now."

Mochaba said, "This is a better coffee bean, Rodolfo. This aroma is great."

A very short time passed, and the pleasant aroma went beyond the castle walls and throughout the kingdom. Mochaba glanced out of one of the open windows of the kitchen and noticed some of his people raising their noses high, evidently sniffing the air, and then inhaling deeply to draw in this wonderful, new aroma. Their satisfied expressions showed how much they liked it. The scent of this freshly roasted coffee soon encircled Munndora and continued traveling further and then even a great distance beyond.

Two long days and nights after the ship's arrival went by with no Lecheenuss in sight. Mochaba and Rodolfo worked tirelessly in making that perfect coffee. At one point, Mochaba thought, *Why not add some flavoring to this new roast? It needs a flavor, but what should it be?* So he got creative and added cocoa and cinnamon to it. At times, they would take breaks to relax. The king would walk to one of the windows to see if his queen was in sight while the days and nights kept building in number. All the time, he kept Lecheenuss's crown, which he had retrieved, close to his heart. They continued adjusting the blend of beans, knowing Marieka was a master in horticulture. The right combination for this coffee would soon be found.

Suddenly, a lady and a man hurried up to one of the open windows of the room where Mochaba was making the coffee and asked what that delightful aroma was that led them there. They said that it seemed to call them, to have them follow it, and this was where the scent had brought them. Soon there were quite a number of people there. All of them asked to come in and have a cup of this magical blend of dark roasted coffee. This told Rodolfo and King Mochaba they had finally found the perfect blend. The taste was delicious, a dark roast, not too strong and with just a touch of mint leaf, cocoa, and cinnamon. They both hoped the queen would also be drawn by the scent and show up soon. King Mochaba made sure this final combination would never be lost and wrote the recipe down. The fragrance attracted many people to the castle. Soon, Rodolfo was giving everyone a cup of this delicious roasted blend.

Wiping the sweat from his brow, the king suddenly yelled to Rodolfo, "We're running out of cinnamon!"

He replied, "It's on the way, My King. I'll go to the supply cabinet. Be right back."

That evening, a warm summer breeze carried the magical aroma to where the queen lay asleep. Early the next morning, Lecheenuss slowly woke up from her darkness. She lay there for only a moment, and when she sat up, she began rubbing the sleep from her eyes.

Confused, she thought, *This is different. Where am I? How did I get here?* She continued rubbing her eyes and running her fingers through her golden hair. From her seated position, she inhaled deeply as she stretched her arms high over her head. Suddenly she noticed a pleasant scent in the air. Lecheenuss relaxed her arms and dropped them while closing her eyes for a quick moment. She thought, *Hmmm, I like that smell. I wonder where it's coming from. Well, time to get up now, I guess.* After she rubbed her eyes again, she opened them and then saw that she had company—a little rabbit had watched her wake up. With a smile of happiness, she said to it, "Good morning, my little friend. I hope you have a good day."

Now ready, she stood up and began walking, following the enchanted fragrance.

Feeling strong now, she walked with confident steps following the aroma she had never known before. It became sweeter as she followed it, and in a short while, Lecheenuss could see the castle. She smiled. Her home was so near, and she was so happy seeing it so close. Lecheenuss didn't know how long she had been away or where she had been. All she knew was that this new fragrance was leading her back to her home, closer to her husband, whom she wanted to hug with her love.

Meanwhile, confident that this was the perfect brew to rescue the queen, Rodolfo took a long walk to relax after serving coffee to the people of Munndora. He had not slept or eaten well in days. While he walked and breathed in the sweet aroma of that coffee fragrance, he came to the forest and thought, *Could Lecheenuss be here?* Even as tired as he was, he thought that was a good possibility and decided to enter. While wandering through the forest, Rodolfo suddenly slipped on a rock, and as he fell to the ground, he hurt one of his knees. He stayed there for a moment rubbing it, and in a few short minutes, he realized the pain wasn't so bad. Another minute passed, and he slowly stood up.

Suddenly, he heard something close by him and thought it might be the queen. Not quite standing up all the way yet, he looked over and saw a woman. Rodolfo was overcome by her beauty, and he told her so. Just then, he fell to his knees again, faint from hunger and a painful knee.

At this, the heart of this woman grew and grew. It was Jayabella, and she forgot all the jealousy she had felt for the queen, her sister. She felt joy in her heart that she had never known before. Finally, here was someone who loved her as she was. That feeling was stronger than anything she had ever experienced. She helped him get up and took him to her house and fed him a wonderful meal, showing him kindness beyond any she had ever shown to another human being. He helped make her feel the love she had never known.

* * *

Still at the castle, King Mochaba took another break and poured himself a cup. He began to pace slowly in his kitchen with positive thoughts of his queen. At one of the windows of that room, he stopped and looked in the distance. A few minutes had passed, and he took another sip. In that distance, Mochaba saw a figure walking in a way he recognized. He thought, *Could it be?* With a squint of his eyes, he tried to see more clearly and then shouted, "SHE'S HERE! That's Lecheenuss. My Lecheenuss! **Lecheenuss!**"

So excited, Mochaba dropped his cup while he ran out of the room. He ignored the tiredness he felt in his legs as he ran to her, all the while repeating her name, "Lecheenuss, Lecheenuss. You're here." In no time, he was outside running to her.

Lecheenuss saw him, and now they both were running to each other. Finally, they embraced. They both laughed with tears of joy in their eyes and said to each other, "Oh, I missed you. I love you."

The spell was broken forever.

Mochaba and Lecheenuss slowly walked back to the castle and into the kitchen. There, the king handed her a cup of that magical blend that had found her and broken the spell. The moment the sweet, hot liquid touched her lips, the clouds lifted from her eyes even more. The king reached under his vest and placed her crown where it belonged, on top of her beautiful long flowing hair. With a big smile, she whispered to him, "I love you, my king."

* * *

King Mochaba was so happy Lecheenuss was home again and safe from all the fearful thoughts he had imagined. The whole kingdom was happy and wanted to celebrate the safe return of their queen.

Mochaba asked Lecheenuss if she felt that would be all right with her. Showing him a bright smile, she said she would like seeing everyone again. She asked if she could have it on the green meadow she liked so much near the water by the east wall of their kingdom. With devoted love for his queen, Mochaba agreed that would be the perfect place to have it and said he would start the arrangements the following day.

Lecheenuss walked closer to Mochaba and gave him a loving hug.

Not saying any more words, she and Mochaba left the room and walked to their bed chambers. They slept peacefully that night knowing they were together again.

The next morning, the king and queen were awakened by the joyful melodies of birds singing. They got up and started getting ready for their day. Mochaba said he would make some coffee for them before he left to meet with some of his people. She agreed with him, and he went to the kitchen and started the fire. Lecheenuss walked in a few minutes later, and while the water heated for their coffee, they both talked about their plans for the day. Breve was going to have Herb and some of his men help set up a gathering of people in the square near Daniel and Kylie's market. The coffee was ready, and they continued making plans as they sipped the delicious brew.

Finished with having their coffee, Mochaba kissed Lecheenuss and said he would be at the market in a couple of hours and he would meet her there. Lecheenuss agreed, and Mochaba started his day. Lecheenuss stayed at the castle so she could talk with her servants and plan a few things she felt were necessary for their home and for the kingdom's celebration. After her directions were given, she left the castle and walked to Marieka's garden to visit with Jana for a little while and arranged to have some items ready for the celebration too. Later that morning, all plans had been made, and after visiting with Jana, the queen went to the market and there visited with some of her people while she waited for Mochaba.

After a short while, Mochaba walked in the market and talked with people there too. Soon most everyone knew of the celebration, and Daniel and Kylia too said they would be happy to supply food for them all. It was early afternoon when King Mochaba and Queen Lecheenuss said their goodbyes to everyone and left to go home.

All plans had been made, and after returning home, the king and queen decided to just relax and spend the rest of the day by a warm, comfortable fire together for a change and enjoy the dreams of the true spirit of love they had together with a peaceful night of rest and sleep.

At sunrise the following morning, everyone came to the grassy meadow ready to celebrate their lives of truth. King Mochaba set up a table to try out his new gift, the coffee maker Rodolfo had brought for him. Queen Lecheenuss began serving that delicious brew to her people and loved visiting with all of them. A short while after the king started blending his new coffee recipe, Rodolfo came and walked towards the queen. She handed him a cup of the delicious brew and with an expression of thankfulness and appreciation for helping her and Mochaba, she said,

"Here is a cup of that delicious coffee you brought for us, Rodolfo. I want you to know that both my husband and I are so grateful that you came to Munndora when you did. All our people are grateful to you.

And thank you for that beautiful table you made for me. My husband thanks you for it too, and he likes the new coffee maker you brought for us. It's easy making coffee now."

"Yes, cousin Mochaba was so afraid that he had lost you, Lecheenuss. I'm so happy I came when I did. Are you all right now, My Queen?"

"Oh yes, Rodolfo, I feel good now, thank you." After a quick second of calm, Lecheenuss said. "My sister talks about you a lot. She wants to ask you something, but she's afraid to. I think I know what it is, though. I've never seen her as happy as she is now. She's changed. My sister really likes you, Rodolfo. Is it a safe voyage to get where everyone is now?"

"Yes it is, My Queen, and it's only a two-day journey. They're all pretty happy being where they are and have cleared some land for planting crops, but the land for developing other orchards is limited. We all agree more land is needed and where they are limits their choices. They all want to develop the business for international trade. Now and again, Breve and Siena have talked with Raphael and Marieka about that, and interesting plans are being made. The voyage to the new land in the Pacific might happen, but the harvest they are doing right now is the important priority. They're working the land they have now, but it may become their second port and used like their plans for Munndora. It is being talked about, but nothing is definite yet."

With a look of interest on her face, Lecheenuss let her other questions rest. She smiled to Rodolfo, and with a friendly wink to him, she turned and continued serving coffee to her people.

Thinking about what Lecheenuss had said about her sister, Rodolfo stood there a couple of minutes while he sipped from his cup. He finished his coffee and left, deciding to walk around the castle grounds hoping Jayabella would be there.

Not knowing that Lecheenuss had spoken to Rodolfo, Jayabella was just sitting alone in a chair by Marieka's garden, puzzled in her thinking of what she should do.

Rodolfo saw her and walked over to her. He reached his hand to her as she stood and with a smile said, "Jayabella, will you walk with me? Let's go to where your sister and Mochaba and everyone are."

His suggestion was a pleasant surprise for her, and she gladly accepted. With a happy feeling they both had, they started talking together as they walked. On the way there, they stopped at the coffee stand. Rodolfo asked the coffee vendor for two cups of the new roasted blend. He gave Jayabella a cup, and she sipped. The moment she drank from her cup, she smiled. Gradually a beautiful glow of happiness shined brightly all around her. She professed her love for Rodolfo.

Forever changed by the love she had found in meeting him, the bad witch Jayabella the Jealous became the good witch Jayabella the Joyful, helping all who had broken hearts find their long-lost love, reminding all that everyone has a special someone out there who will love him or her for who he or she really is.

Rodolfo and Jayabella walked from the coffee stand to the beach where the people were celebrating. They both talked about their lives and what they had lived through. With a soft, gentle voice, she asked Rodolfo if he would be leaving soon.

He saw a tear fall from her eye as she asked that question and her bright glow begin to fade. Rodolfo reached to her, and they stopped. He hugged her softly, looking deep into her eyes. With a short pause, he said to her, "Yes, I will be going back soon, Jayabella."

The love she had in her heart for him was strong. Silently she searched her thoughts to try to find the words she wanted to say but couldn't find them. The quiet sadness she felt started making her tears fall freely from her eyes now. She quickly lowered her head, and the fear of losing Rodolfo began to be too real for her. She tried hiding her sad feelings but couldn't. For the first time in her life, Jayabella was afraid, and the feelings of loneliness started to control her emotions. Within just a couple of minutes, the sadness got stronger and then stronger. She kept thinking, *Oh, Rodolfo, please don't leave me.*

Rodolfo was so moved when he saw her shoulders heaving uncontrollably as she began to cry. He pulled her close to him with a loving embrace. Tightly he held her with his warmth of protection and said to her softly with a gentle and loving voice, "Jayabella, shhh . . . wait, shhh, shhh . . . Jayabella, there, there, shhh, Jayabella, shhh, sweetheart, shhh." At these words, she began to relax a little. Rodolfo continued to comfort her. "There, my love. It's okay, hon," They rocked each other slowly for a few minutes, sharing their honest feelings for each other without talking. Jayabella began to calm herself while Rodolfo still held her close to him. He gently rubbed the tears from her eyes with a clean, soft cloth and then handed it to her to keep while gently patting her on her back to help her relax even more. Rodolfo helped lift up her beautiful face so they could look into each other's eyes closely. He smiled to her with a loving care in his eyes that she could see in his soul, and he said, "I have found you, Jayabella. You are the woman of my heart, the treasure of my life. I need you to be with me. I want to grow old with you, Jayabella. Please don't be worried. I will take good care of you. Come with me when we leave Munndora!"

Jayabella became speechless. She felt such a warmth of love being with Rodolfo. She was embarrassed about the way she appeared. But it was as if he already knew what she was thinking, and without saying any words, he just held her closer to show her that everything would be okay. Her gentle glow began to return as she felt that Rodolfo was her real love. She had always known there was someone who would love her, but for whatever reason, she had felt afraid of that. This new feeling was so new and pleasant in her. She felt a happiness she had never known before. Brighter and brighter her glowing warmth appeared. She felt so lucky to have Rodolfo in her life. With emotion from deep inside her heart, Jayabella said, "I love you, my prince. I will always love you, Rodolfo."

With joy in their eyes, they hugged each other tightly.

Having seen this exchange, the king and queen took a break from serving coffee and walked over to the couple. Lecheenuss reached to her sister's hand, asking Rodolfo if he would let her talk with Jayabella a little while. He readily agreed, and as the two sisters walked away, Mochaba said to Rodolfo, "Now that the girls are talking, let's plan our next shipment."

Rodolfo replied, "Sure thing, My King. The ship's close by, and I have work to do and inventory to take before we leave. Let's plan it all there."

As they walked, the king asked, "Rodolfo, my queen said there is some talk about all of you taking a long voyage to that body of land in the Pacific Ocean. Is that true?"

Rodolfo replied, "Yes, they're talking about it but that's all. There are no definite plans being made right now."

King Mochaba said, "That is interesting they talk about it. What will they do with the property they have?"

"I don't know, My King. It's just talk for now. I did hear that, if they do decide to go, then the land they are at right now may be used the same way they want to use Munndora—as a harbor for supplies and export."

The king was quiet for a second and then said, "Let me know when things begin to change. Would you do that for me, Rodolfo?"

"Of course."

"How are Marieka and Raphael?" the king continued with his questions.

"Everyone is doing well," Rodolfo replied.

"Marieka sure has made a good impression on the people here," the king said, "and probably in the kingdoms we do business with. What's her secret for the crops she grows and improving the supplies that come here from other lands we do business with? I know she doesn't grow the coffee beans yet, but how does she do it? She makes a masterpiece with that product."

"Marieka has her secrets," Rodolfo answered with a smile. "She said that you and Lecheenuss should come over and maybe she'll share some with you both."

"Hmm. We just might do that," the king said.

Rodolfo added, "There's some talk about increasing the amount of supplies they want to ship, though. It's not the greatest news. They're finding out that they're limited by how much land they have right now. Breve's planning something, though, I think."

"Hmm. More secrets? We will have to visit them," the king said and then added, "I see their strength in you, Rodolfo. I am so glad you made it here when you did. Lecheenuss and I both want you and your crew to know that you're all welcome here anytime. All of you! By the way, Rodolfo, the queen is so happy about the table you made for her. That rosewood table is beautiful! Did that take you a long time to make? The craftsmanship is excellent."

Rodolfo replied, "I'm happy Lecheenuss likes the table, Mochaba. It was no problem doing that for her. Siena ordered the shipment of that rosewood and mentioned that she wanted to give Lecheenuss something special. I made it for the love I have for you both. The timing couldn't have been more perfect for us to get here. We were a couple of days off schedule, but we made it. Things turned out well, didn't they, My King?"

Relieved with how everything had turned out and having his queen back home safe, Mochaba agreed and said, "Sure did, Rodolfo! Sure did."

At the vessel, Rodolfo positioned the gangplank, and both walked aboard talking about the days ahead. Mochaba said, "I forgot to tell you that your father came by the castle a while ago for a visit. He asked if we knew when your shipment would be here."

When they stepped on the main deck, Rodolfo said, "Yes, I'll be going over there to see him later today. See how he's doing. Hey, have a seat. I need to get the logbook and will be right back."

Before sitting down, the king walked around the deck for a while. He heard a scratching noise like a small rodent would make followed by a faint chirping. Mochaba thought that was a little peculiar, especially because he wasn't familiar with the sounds. *Ah, it must be a mouse. Bound to have one or more aboard, I guess.* He looked around for it but didn't see it. He continued looking and bent down with his ear close to the deck where he thought he had heard it.

Rodolfo came back and saw Mochaba listening for something. As he sat down on one of the steps on deck and opened his logbook, Rodolfo said, "Glad I put it up where I did. For a minute, I thought our little mascot might have chewed it up. Hey, Mochaba, what are you trying to find? Did you drop something?"

Surprised by Rodolfo's appearance, Mochaba said, "Oh, hi, Rodolfo. No, I heard a sound. It got my attention, and I thought I'd try to find out what it was."

"Oh, was it a quiet, sort of chirping sound? A bit of scratching noise with it?"

Mochaba nodded.

"That's our stowaway."

"Stowaway?" Mochaba asked. "I thought it was a rodent or something."

"Yes," Rodolfo said, "stowaway. He's our little mascot. Every ship needs one. He snuck aboard before we left the port."

Rodolfo went to the area where King Mochaba had heard the sounds. It took a few minutes to catch the little guy, but he soon did. He gently grabbed the little critter, carried it to where Mochaba was sitting, and said, "Here he is, My King. You'll find he is a friendly little guy."

Mochaba said, "Ah, a rabbit. How'd he get aboard?"

Rodolfo pulled a carrot out of one of the small sacks where they were sitting and gave it to the little friend. While feeding it, he said, "I think your sister put him here for us. Anyway, it's not bad having one on board."

Rodolfo continued talking with Mochaba and explained that the next shipment to Munndora would include tea, along with the other supplies. He said a special orchard was being worked and tea would be harvested soon from that area they are working on right now. Business was good, he said, but could be better. During their talk, Rodolfo showed a map he and Breve had drawn of their new place. Breve wanted Mochaba to have this chart and thought that one day he and Lecheenuss might come and see them.

"Sounds great, Rodolfo," Mochaba replied. "It'll be awhile, though, before we can do that. When you make it home, give our respects to everyone and especially our love to Mother and Father. By the way, I know you made a difference in Jayabella's life. Cousin, we all feel you found a champion. Lecheenuss told me she was going to have girl talk with her, whatever that means. But I know it's something good, Rodolfo."

Rodolfo said, "We both talked about some things already. She'll be going with me."

King Mochaba turned to him and said, "With what Lecheenuss said earlier to me, cousin, we know that Jayabella will be happy going with you. I'm glad you both found each other, Rodolfo."

There was silence for a few moments, and King Mochaba added, "Well, I have some duties back home to take care of, and you have some here too, it looks like, so we'll see you tomorrow. Thank you for this map. Lecheenuss will be glad to have it too. We'll come and see you before your ship leaves. Tell Herb hi for me too when you see him, and Rodolfo, thank you for helping me find my wife. You will be missed. See you tomorrow, cousin."

"Thank you too, cousin Mochaba, My King. See you and Lecheenuss later."

Mochaba walked down the gangplank and on to the castle.

Rodolfo stayed seated where he was and spent the next fifteen minutes or so writing down the important facts about the cargo his ship had brought to Munndora. When he finished, he folded shut the logbook and got up to put it away for safe keeping. The mascot followed him for a little ways, and Rodolfo picked it up and carried him to the enclosed room that he and his crew had made for the little guy on this last trip.

He spent several minutes walking around on deck to double check everything he wanted when some of his crew walked up the gangplank to spend their tired evening aboard ship. Rodolfo welcomed them and continued his survey on deck. To his satisfaction, all things were put away in their proper places, organized, and arranged in his systematic way.

It was still daylight when he completed this informal inspection and then walked down the gangplank and away from the docks to where he knew his father would still be at that time of day, the kingdom's marketplace. When Rodolfo got there, he saw Queen Lecheenuss and Jana talking together. As he walked up to them, he looked around and saw Herb helping Daniel towards the back of the market sorting some fish on one of the shelves in a display booth.

Changing his direction, Rodolfo went directly over to see his father. Daniel saw Rodolfo's approach first and caught Rodolfo off guard as he yelled, "Wild salmon in the air!" He heaved the salmon to Rodolfo, and it flew in a fast flight.

With eyes opened very wide, Rodolfo stopped instantly and caught the fish in both hands, and with a smile, he held it high saying, "This is the first time I've gone fishing and caught one in the first two minutes. I'll come here more often." He lowered it down so he could set it on the counter to wrap it and said, "Thank you, Daniel."

Herb and Daniel came to him with happy cheer in their voices. Herb reached his arms out to give him a hug and said, "Welcome back, son. How long will you be staying?"

As Herb got some paper to wrap the fish, Rodolfo said, "We plan on leaving port tomorrow, Father. Our next shipment, though, will have us back in three months. Lieutenant Vincent is supervising a small load of cargo right now that we'll be taking back for Marieka, and then we'll have to go back. Breve and Siena both give you their love."

Herb felt some tender sadness hearing that, but he understood the situation about all that had happened since his son had come to port. To Daniel, he said, "I'm going to spend the rest of the day with my son. Okay with you I do that?"

With a smile and a wave to them, Daniel replied, "Sure is, Herb. Good seeing you, Rodolfo. Come back again."

Raising the wrapped salmon, Rodolfo said again, "Thanks, Daniel."

Father and son walked outside to the wagon Herb had brought to town that day. They got on it, Herb grabbed the reins, and they rode to Herb's place, talking and laughing together as good families do. It took almost an hour.

When they arrived, Rodolfo handed his father the salmon and said right away, "I'll take care of the wagon for you and get the horses ready for the night."

Herb got down off the wagon and said, "Good idea, son. I'll get this ready," and he walked in his house with the salmon.

Rodolfo rode the wagon to the stable, got down to unhitch the horses, removed all the harness gear, and walked them to their stalls. He left the wagon under the eave's cover where he had parked it and then walked to the house.

Herb got the fire burning, and Rodolfo walked to the seat he knew well and sat down. He removed his shoes and just sat back and relaxed.

After Herb put the salmon on the stove, he got a couple of cups and filled them with some fresh juice that he had brought from the market the day before. He brought one of the cups over to Rodolfo and placed it on a table near the seat. Herb said, "I'm glad you're safe, son. Everyone in town misses all of you. It's good seeing you again. Here, son. I got this yesterday from Kylia." Herb walked back to watch the salmon cook, and Rodolfo joined him. They talked about changes in the kingdom—all the improvements to the roads, the increase of stockpiles, and more.

Herb asked how Breve and Siena were with their new home. Rodolfo answered, "They like the area they chose. It has plenty of water, and their land is rich with minerals for growing certain foods and plants, but Breve found out that the three orchards Marieka and Raphael started won't be enough for the bigger plans they have. They wanted more to happen by now, and they're finding out they're limited and won't be able to get more land now. They are talking about the land Raphael spoke of some time ago located in the Pacific."

Herb said, "Oh, they're all talking about that? I remember when Breve was concerned about that new land. He said that Raphael and Marieka thought to go there and see if the land was as plentiful and abundant as they had been told it was. Interesting. That started to make me think about it too. I was curious about it. I mean, that could be a good discovery, but it is so far away." Herb removed the salmon from the fire and placed it on top of the vegetables he had prepared on a tray.

Rodolfo said, "Mmm, that smells good. I've always liked the food you cook."

"You cook good food too, son. Let's go sit down."

Herb carried the tray to his table while Rodolfo got their cups and filled them with more juice. When they sat down, Herb gave his thanks for having his son back in Munndora safe and healthy. Rodolfo added his thanks for the guidance back to Munndora. Then they started their supper and continued talking. Rodolfo mentioned how the queen was doing since she had found her way back to the castle and how happy she and King Mochaba were.

When they had their last bite, Herb said in a humble voice, "Rodolfo, your room is the way you left it when you went to the new property. I'm so glad you are safe and could be here to visit with me."

"I'm glad I came here too, Father. You look a little tired. I'll clean up. Have you been okay working the apple orchards?"

"Oh yes, Rodolfo. I've hired a few extra men, and things are pretty good. No worries. You look a little tired too."

"Yes, I have been doing quite a bit these past few days. Will you be able to take me back to the docks tomorrow morning? I met someone, Father, and I want you to meet her."

"I'm happy for you, Rodolfo. I look forward to meeting her, maybe tomorrow. I'm meeting with Mochaba after I get you to the docks. He mentioned just the other day that he might go over to see Breve soon. Asked if I wanted to go too. I'm sure glad Lecheenuss made it back home safe. It'll be good seeing her tomorrow too." Herb got up off his chair slowly and said, "Well, I think I'm going to bed now. Thanks for cleaning up. It's been a long day for me. Make yourself at home, son. See you in the morning. I love you. Good night."

"I love you too, Father. Thank you for the delicious supper. Good night. See you tomorrow."

After a few moments of thought, Rodolfo got up from his seat, walked to the table, and picked up all the dishes to clean them. After washing everything, he made a quiet moment. He closed his eyes and said, "Thank you, Father." Then he opened his eyes, walked directly to his old room, and in no time at all, fell into a deep sleep.

The next morning, Rodolfo was awakened by a pleasing, familiar fragrance in the air. He said to himself, "Hot cakes. Oh boy." Rodolfo quickly got out of bed, got dressed, walked to the kitchen, and saw his father in the middle of cooking some flapjacks.

He said to Rodolfo, "I bet you're ready for a hearty breakfast. Grab a plate. There's bacon and some eggs over there, and these two cakes are just about ready for you."

Rodolfo smiled and said, "Thank you. I'll get your plate too."

Ready to sit down, Rodolfo set both plates on the table. Herb brought two cups of coffee, and while he set those on the table, he said, "I think you'll like this brew, son." Then Herb sat down, and they started their breakfast and talked about the day's responsibilities before the ship left Munndora.

With the hour being early still as they finished their meal, Rodolfo said he would hitch the horses to the wagon and get it ready for them to go and start their day. Herb said that it was already done and they could leave when they both were ready to go.

Soon they were in the wagon and riding to town.

They got to the docks when the lieutenant and crew were just about finished with the light cargo that they were shipping back.

Rodolfo climbed down off the wagon and said he would help his crew and do the inventory while things were being loaded. Herb said that he was going to the castle now to meet with King Mochaba and that they both would be back soon. He rode the rest of the way and parked the wagon at the stables to walk and meet with Mochaba.

For the next three hours, all cargo was put onboard and inventory was completed. The ship would be ready to go at any time now. Rodolfo gave the lieutenant and the ship's crew some time to take care of their personal needs in town before they left and told them all to be back onboard in two hours and ready to ship out.

Rodolfo saw captain Tyrus organizing a crew for one of the other ships at the docks and walked over to talk with him and ask him a few questions. When the captain finished communicating with that crew, Rodolfo walked up to him wishing him a good day, and they discussed matters about Rodolfo's ship. During the end of their conversation, they turned their attention to King Mochaba and Queen Lecheenuss as they rode on horseback to the docks. Rodolfo saw following behind them his father, and in the wagon with him was Jayabella.

Rodolfo and the captain walked over to Mochaba and Lecheenuss as they dismounted, and the four of them waited till Herb's wagon got there too. They all saw Jayabella's big smile as the wagon came to a stop and she and Herb got down from it. Everyone talked together as families do and were all happy to see each other together like that. Herb and Queen Lecheenuss walked to the back of the wagon to get the few personal items that the queen had gotten for Jayabella to take with her, much to Jayabella's surprise.

Herb handed those items to his son and said, "Rodolfo, I've met your new friend, Jayabella. She and Queen Lecheenuss were part of that meeting we had this morning, and they helped us a lot with their questions and answers. King Mochaba and I are so happy for you to be with this lady. She is such a nice person and, as I said, has some definite ideas. Queen Lecheenuss and she added to the solutions in our meeting."

They were still talking an hour later when some of the ship's crew started coming back and, with the captain's help, began to get their vessel ready to ship out. Soon the last two crewmembers and Lieutenant Vincent came, and all was being readied for their voyage.

Herb reached to his son to give him a loving pat on his back and said, "Your mother would be proud of you, son. You and Jayabella, please be safe. Take good care of each other. I love you both. Tell Breve and Siena we all miss them."

"I'll do that, Father."

King Mochaba and Queen Lecheenuss walked over to Rodolfo and Jayabella, and Mochaba said, "We are happy you found each other. You will both be missed. Tell Marieka and Raphael that the cargo is well organized thanks to Jana's knowledge of the business. We know she is the right person to oversee having their crops delivered here. Give our love to the rest of our family."

Rodolfo reached down and got Jayabella's items and said, "Thank you too, all of you. I'm so glad I got here when I did, My King. Queen Lecheenuss, I am happy you are safe, and thank you for knowing Jayabella's heart and helping us find each other. Please be safe, all of you. I had better get these aboard for you now, Jayabella. See you in a minute."

Jayabella began to show some tears of a loving happiness when she reached to hug the king and queen. She said, "I'm so thankful to both of you. You've helped me see many things more clearly than I ever did before. I am so thankful you have forgiven me, sister, My Queen. I love you both very much." With a loving, tender embrace, she reached to them again and repeated, "Thank you. I love you. Please be safe. I better go now."

She walked up the gangplank and soon was aboard. Rodolfo met with her on deck, and they both turned to the royal couple and his father. Soon the vessel began to slowly leave the docks. Rodolfo and Jayabella waved their goodbyes, and the others waved back to them, watching as the ship began to float away. Soon the ship's sails were down, and a gentile summer breeze filled them as the vessel continued through the bay on its voyage. The king and queen and Herb continued watching as the ship floated farther into the distance, and in only a few minutes, it could no longer be seen from the docks. Herb turned his attention to the royal couple and said, "Please tell me if you need my help with anything. I love you both." Before they departed from each other, they each gave a brief hug and said their goodbyes.

Soon, only the captain and his two dockhands remained on the docks, bringing another ship to port for unloading its cargo.

* * *

Word went out far and wide of the healing powers in Munndora and that it would be the main port receiving all shipments of the special coffee from the new land. People traveled from miles around to sample it. The rich paid handsomely for the supplies coming to Munndora and returned to their homelands. The bags of coffee Mochaba had received soon were  depleted, and he could see that his sister would have to produce much more. Her new orchards would not be able to supply enough product to keep everyone happy. *How long*, he wondered, *before Marieka and the others in their new location would consider their attempt to find that other mysterious land in the Pacific?*

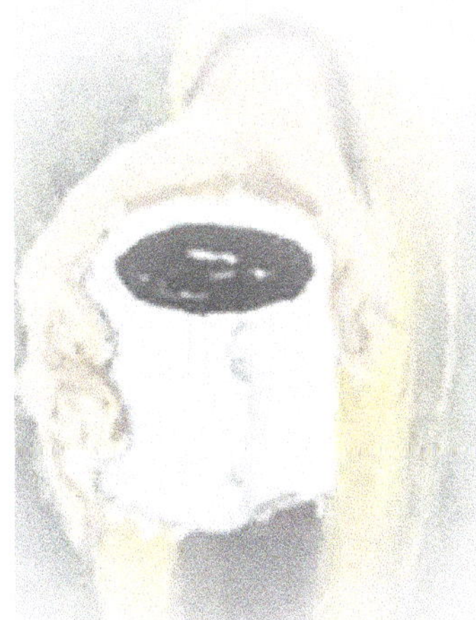

For now, the king put such thoughts aside and was happy with the success of this new brew. Mochaba used all proceeds from the sale of this coffee to build more schools, more paths, and better roads for his people.

Now everyone the world over knows of the healing power of love and great coffee. No one was in want of anything. Love and romance embraced the whole land. Happy again was the land of Munndora.

The voyage will continue.

"See you soon."

Acknowledgements

Thank you Gary and Jana, Bill and Freda, Eli, Debbie, Bob, Dave, and the many others for knowing and living the truth of good, honest friendship and offering encouragement to help others.